Search Through Pirate's Alley

by

Mildred Houghton Comfort

Illustrations by

Anne Fleur

New York - 1945

WILLIAM MORROW AND CO.

Published, November, 1945
Second printing, April, 1946
Third printing, October, 1949

PRINTED IN THE UNITED STATES

To
Emily Sue Patton
of
The French Quarter
of New Orleans

Contents

Contents

Off and On with Jackson's Head

THE small door in the big green gate of the D'Orsay house on Royal Street opened and closed with an inrush of hurry and an outrush of scurry. A large piece of pinkish plaster on the street wall, long since loosened, fell away and revealed the soft, old brick of chrome-orange underneath. Years ago, when the French Quarter *was* New Orleans and the Garden District had not even been dreamed of, it would have mattered. Now, in 1900, nobody noticed, for the glories of the *Vieux Carré,* or Old Square, had faded even for many New Orleaneans.

All morning long the tradesmen shuffled in from the street along the narrow passageway of damp herringbone brick, and then shuffled out again, with Mammy Margot's voice chasing after them. Charcoal from the street vendor! A freezer of ice cream from Chretiéns! A great basket of groceries from Solari's.

Pierre D'Orsay stopped trying to study. For three hours he had been sitting and fidgeting at his desk in the garçonnière, the wing of the house where he and his uncle had their rooms. He was twelve-going-on-thirteen and he felt a great responsibility about his work. If he could enter the Academy in the spring, with a scholarship, it would mean a great deal to his family; especially if it were true that his father had lost a great deal of money recently when something went wrong at the bank. Pierre didn't quite understand the details about bank stock and bank failures but he knew that it meant trouble. He felt a strange tenseness and excitement in the air, and with all that confusion below, his mind just would not stay indoors with his books.

He stepped out on his own galerie and glanced down into the flowery patio and stretched his arms in the sunlight. He looked as if he belonged in the outdoors: sturdy and strong and so eager for action. It was amazing how well he fenced, how swiftly he could gallop over the plantation on a spirited horse, and what a hearty appetite he had. At the sight of Mammy Margot below, shouting at the tradesmen, his dark eyes glowed and he chuckled to himself. Mammy Margot had been with the D'Orsay family for better than two generations and she took care of them with a firm, though ever-loving hand.

"What's going on, Mammy Margot?" Pierre inquired, leaning over the galerie rail of wrought iron lace.

He half expected Mammy to raise her pink palm in a stern, expressive gesture that would send him back into the dim study. But for some reason she didn't feel like scolding him for leaving his books.

"Bless yo' hea't, it's mos' noon," she exclaimed. "Come

on down, honey, an' Mammy'll fix you'n Miss Collette a nice lunch in the patio."

Pierre ran down the outside stairs so lightly and swiftly that he was beside Mammy Margot before she could retreat into the servants' quarters.

"Something's going on, Mammy Margot. What is it? Please."

"Well-bred chillun don't ask questions," Mammy Margot chided. "But I's tellin' yo' private-lak' dat we ain't none of us goin' to be happy anywheres but heah."

With a wide sweep of her arm she took in the D'Orsay establishment.

"Of course not," Pierre soothed. "If we didn't live here, where else *could* we live? This is our house. Why should we ever move?"

Mammy Margot did not answer, but she mumbled, "Yas, sah, heah in dis house wha' yo' chillun was bo'n."

Collette, her hair still in rag curlers that her aunts called *couettes,* screeched down the stairway from the main rooms of the house and catapulted herself into Mammy's arms. Mammy gave her a quick hug and hustled inside to get their lunch. Collette turned to her brother.

"Guess what, Pierre! We are both to sit at the family table tonight for dinner. Mama says we are old enough to sit in on family conferences, and Papa agrees, especially when it's something about our home."

"You've been listening at keyholes," Pierre accused, surprised that Collette seemed to know more than he did.

"I don't have to," Collette declared, flouncing about, "not

when I keep my ears open anyway. Pierre, do you suppose we're going to have to live in some other house?"

"Where did you get *that* idea?" Pierre inquired sharply. It made his throat tight to hear her say that, especially after the hints Mammy Margot had given him.

"Well, Mama said to Papa," Collette reported, "'Don't worry; if the worst comes to the worst, we can always sell this Royal Street house.'"

"Stop talking nonsense," Pierre ordered and kept opening and shutting his fists. "Selling our house is a lot to worry about, and she wouldn't say 'don't worry' and talk about selling in the same breath."

"Maybe she didn't say that exactly," Collette conceded. "I hope I'm wrong."

Their talk was interrupted when they heard footsteps coming in through the runway leading from the street. Collette ran over and crouched behind a potted camellia to hide her *couettes*. A tall, thick gentleman whose striped trousers and brown leather portmanteau gave him a most official look was being escorted by Mammy's grandson, Toby, up into the living quarters.

"Why, that's Monsieur Gustav La Branche," Pierre discovered.

But what would Grandpère D'Orsay's lawyer be doing here?

Grandpère D'Orsay had died ten years ago, so Pierre hardly remembered him. But just thinking about him made Pierre shiver with a strange delight, for Grandpère had had a life filled with adventures. It wasn't easy to get his grandmother or Papa to tell about Grandpère D'Orsay, but the children did know that even when he was just a boy, Grandpère had had an important part in the monarchist plot to rescue Napoleon from St. Helena and bring him to New Orleans.

Pierre and Collette were still standing soberly, looking after the dignified Monsieur La Branche when Mammy Margot called them to the table, set up in the patio. They were busily eating their gumbo when Mama came hurrying out.

"Bon jour," she said, kissing them hastily. "We are very busy today, as you see. I'm afraid that Mammy Margot won't be able to take Collette promenading on Esplanade Boulevard this afternoon. Pierre, would you like to take her over to Jackson Park to play?"

"Of course I'll like it," Pierre agreed, but he could not resist the question that was on the tip of his tongue. "Mama, is it true that we may sell our Royal Street house?"

Mama always faced Pierre with a straight and shining look. She had eyes the color of deep blue violets, and there was a great deal of gold light in her dark hair. To look at her one would not dream what a capable person she was.

"We shall depend on you," she said, "to help us find a way to solve our problem," then added graciously, with a little formal bow as though he were a grown-up, "Your presence, cheri, is requested at dinner."

"Thank you, Mama. Collette told me that we were both to be with the family at dinner. Will she be a help, too?"

"She will be decorative," said Mama, twinkling.

Collette tossed her rag curlers and laughed impishly.

A little later the chocolate brown curls were free of their *couettes* and graced by a large, perky bow of stiff blue ribbon. In her beautifully starched and ironed frock Collette rustled along Royal Street beside Pierre.

"Let's cross through Pirate's Alley for good luck," she suggested.

"We'll need it." Pierre worried. "I wish we knew what Mama meant by 'our problem.' "

"We might as well enjoy playing until we do," Collette decided, practically. "Come on!"

They came out through Pirate's Alley between the gray walls of the Cabildo and the Cathedral. Across the street, before them, stood Jackson Square, surrounded by a handsome iron fence and hemmed in on two sides by the Pontalba Apartments with their lacy galeries. Pierre stared happily at the tropical trees and late flowers, but Collette had already discovered half a dozen school friends who lived in the Royal Street neighborhood.

Soon the D'Orsay children were playing "hide the ball," racing around the equestrian statue of General Jackson and shrilling past the benches where old men read their newspapers. Pierre played mechanically, his mind on the D'Orsay house. He watched with amusement when the ball that Collette had hidden in a most obvious place, a palm tree, came bouncing out.

Then for a long time it was very interesting because the

ball remained in the crotch of a camphor tree whose gray bark served as protective coloring. After that someone tucked it away in the base of a little statue near the bamboo thicket beside the Decatur Street fence. Finally Pierre lost interest in the game. Troubled and unhappy, he stood looking at some late roses.

He was roused suddenly when Collette and the others began to shout, "Pierre can't find the ball; Pierre can't find the ball!"

He was the only one who had not won the privilege of hiding the ball. It was plainly his turn.

"Yes, I can, and I will, too," he called back.

Alert now, he ran here and there, striving to find a new place where the last winner might have placed the ball. No one had used the clump of oleanders across from the Cabildo. He rushed into the dense shade, and at first he could see nothing. But he quickly became accustomed to the shadows, and there, cleverly propped between the iron palings, was the ball.

Pierre returned to the players, the ball in his hands. He felt its round hardness and swung his arm in a circle, as he had seen professional ball players do. The children accepted his signal, their hands over their eyes. Suddenly he had an idea. Why not send the ball sailing into the sky, to find its own hiding place?

His eyes squinted into the sunlight and closed on the ecstasy of that beautiful swing. He hurled with all his might.

Crash! His eyes batted open! He became, almost instantly, the center of a whirlpool of cries and shouts.

In chagrin he saw what had happened. The ball, spinning through the air, had made a direct hit on General Jackson's head and knocked it off. The horror of it chilled his spine. He was so filled with shame that he wanted to run and hide in the bamboo thicket. Instead, he stepped automatically forward, his face flushed. The others stood behind him, silently staring at the headless statue.

Pierre saw the finely wrought iron head outside the enclosure where it had rattled down. It was being guarded by Collette; and, unbelievably, Collette was laughing.

"Pierre knocked off General Jackson's head!" she shouted. "That was more than General Butler could do!"

A guard and a couple of policemen rushed up, and then a band of gypsies and Sicilians from the docks joined the crowd.

"Who did that?" a guard's voice thundered.

"I did, sir," Pierre acknowledged, his face red with embarrassment. "It was an accident."

"What are you going to do about it?" the guard demanded, and now his bulk was augmented by the bulk of other blue-coats with shiny brass buttons and billy clubs.

"I shall replace it, sir," Pierre assured him. His voice squeaked.

"Sure. Let 'im try," a big Irishman urged. "His folks shed blood under Jackson: let *him* get scratched up a bit, if only for the glory of it."

A policeman picked up the metal head with one hand and boosted Pierre unceremoniously over the enclosure fence with the other.

Pierre dropped onto the grass and stood looking up at the stone pedestal. It had never looked very high before; but it took two men to help him scramble on top of it. The statue itself loomed above him as he stood under the belly of the horse and saw the General's leg in the stirrup.

A janitor from the Pontalba Apartments brought a ladder, and while two men held it, Pierre wobbled onto the rungs. He glanced down, almost missed his footing, then deliberately glanced down again. The children were peering up at him, their hands shading their eyes, their mouths tense. They believed he could do it; they had as much faith in him as though he were Old Hickory himself.

He took a deep, shuddery breath. He was as high as he dared go, almost doubled up at the top of the shaking ladder. A guard reached up and steadied his legs with big, firm hands. A policeman handed him the head, saying, "Mischief is always easier to do than to undo," but there was a beloved burr in the chiding.

Pierre held tightly to the head with both hands. His arms ached and his eyes blurred with the effort of trying to slip it on. Sweat ran down his face.

Then, when he least expected it, there was a brief, grating rattle, and the head settled into place.

The crowd cheered and the Cathedral chimes joined in—striking five.

"We've got to hurry," Collette urged when Pierre was again beside her, his hand tight in hers.

Wordlessly they ran back along Pirate's Alley and were

on Royal Street when Collette saw Mammy Margot charging upon them in full sail.

"We're late! What'll we tell her?" Collette worried.

"She herself always warned us that the truth would save a lot of trouble," Pierre advised.

Mammy was spotless in a pure white tignon and apron. Her full dress was so stiffly starched that it rustled like dry leaves in a high wind.

She reserved judgment, as she always did, until she had heard excuses.

"Ah'd lak' to a seed Mastah Pierre," she chuckled, and her laughter shook her whole body. "But yo' 'membah dis, yo' chillun: eff'n yo' do some'in' *good,* yo' *fergits* hit; eff'n yo' does some'in' *bad,* yo' *remembahs!"*

"What if it's good in some ways and bad in others?" Pierre inquired, sliding sidewise along the stucco walls of the houses, and stumbling over the jutting steps, so carefully scrubbed. "It was *bad* when I knocked off General Jackson's head, but it was *good* that I could put it on again."

Mammy Margot gave a satisfied grunt, deep in her throat.

"Mastah Pierre," she prophesied, "yo' is a-goin' to be a avocat. And a avocat is jest what this fambly needs."

"Mammy Margot!" Collette tugged at the hand so firm in hers. "Mayn't I stop in at the Miniature Shop and buy myself a little horse? I've got a penny Mama gave me tied in the corner of my handkerchief."

"Little hoss!" Mammy Margot sniffed. "I should think yo'd had enuff hosses fer one day. We got plenty othah troubles."

Her voice had deepened like organ tones in a Negro spiritual, and she marched Collette past the Miniature Shop without so much as a glance at the fascinating window with all the tiny dolls. Collette knew that Mammy Margot loved the little toys, the dolls and houses and animals quite as much as she did. Something must be seriously wrong.

Glancing sidewise at Mammy Margot, Collette wanted to cry. Nothing, she thought, could be as sad as a sober, round, black face that was so wonderful when it was wreathed in smiles.

"We got fambly troubles," mourned Mammy Margot.

Just at that moment Pierre stumbled over an up-ended flagstone where it had been patched with crumbling brick. He fell, cutting his knee and bruising his shin.

"Oh, Pierre, you're bleeding," Collette cried. "It's a good thing that we're almost home."

The children followed Mammy Margot in through the small door of the big green gate of the D'Orsay house. The brick-laid passageway smelled cool. It was good to be home.

Pierre and Collette stood for a few seconds at the entrance to the patio which was the heart of the big house, then turned to look at each other. Up to this moment they had not admitted, either to themselves or to each other, that the wealth and security they had always known might actually be threatened. But Mammy Margot's face was a barometer of the family fortunes, and never before had she looked so solemn.

No longer, Pierre and Collette realized, could they take home for granted.

Where a Will Is Missing

Mammy Margot snatched Collette off for a cat-nap and a bath before dinner. Pierre limped slowly up the steps of the runway and stood on his own galerie. He noticed that all the white chrysanthemums had been cut, and were ready for the trip to the cemetery on All Saints' Day. The yellow and rust-colored flowers, like late autumn sunshine, remained. Confederate roses and ivy climbed the thick brick walls that enclosed the court; Pierre himself had helped stick pieces of broken glass into the plastered top of the walls to keep stray cats from wandering into this bird sanctuary.

That feathery parkinsonia in front of the dark magnolia had been planted by a mocking bird, so Mammy Margot said, ten years ago when Collette was born. All the fine camellias and azaleas had been set in formal, raised gardens, to be enjoyed for years and years. This wasn't a garden to move away from.

Pierre went into his room and found his clothes laid out on his bed, quite as though he were a grown-up. Laboriously and painfully he took a sponge bath and dressed.

Although there was still an hour before dinner, the lights of the house shone through the fan-shaped windows; and Pierre, feeling lonely, went down into the patio and climbed the winding stairs into the main parlors.

His mother was there, wearing the stiff blue silk dress and the jewels that made her look like a princess. She smelled of the vertivert in which the dress had been packed.

"Come in, cheri," she said. "The rest will soon be here."

Pierre had always thought the double parlors the most beautiful rooms in the world; and tonight they seemed doubly wonderful. They were immense twin rooms, separated by great paneled sliding doors. Only one of the white marble fireplaces, however, was lighted. A small charcoal fire burned in it. The flames warmed the Aubusson carpet with its delicate leaves and vines and roses. It showed up the hand-made curtains of pure Irish handkerchief linen, elaborately embroidered and trimmed with lace. The crystal chandeliers were shot through with millions of rainbows. At the far end of the second parlor stood the graceful, gold-painted chairs and settees that had come over from France at the time of the Revolution.

"Come over here, Pierre," Mama said brightly. "Tell me about your pleasant afternoon. What's the matter, cheri?"

Noticing Pierre's knee, she clucked in motherly fashion and moving briskly over the cypress floors, almost black from years of polishing, she took him up to her bedroom on the second floor.

Mama poured some water in a basin, adding a medicinal-smelling lotion; and while he sat on the hassock that was used to climb into the high four-poster, Mama bathed the knee and bandaged it. To keep from wincing, Pierre counted the repeated acanthus leaves in the handsome rosette in the ceiling.

Back in the parlors, Mama gave him no time for questions, but said, practically, "Pierre, let's make a semicircle

of comfortable chairs for the conclave. The leather chairs for the men—and the satin-upholstered for the women."

Pierre was still arranging chairs and Mama was busy with her embroidery when Tante Bébé arrived.

Tante Bébé was attired in a handsome suit, set off by a feather boa; and her little hat, cocked over one eye, made her look roguish. Tante Bébé, whose real name was Solidelle D'Orsay, was ten years older than her brother, Pierre, the father of Pierre, Junior, and Collette; but she always looked young. The family called her their perennial.

She said hello, then glanced at Pierre's bandaged knee and scratches.

"What under the sun have you been doing?" she inquired. "Kicking garbage pails?"

"Pierre wouldn't do such a thing," Mama defended her son, but her lips turned up at the corners.

"Wouldn't you, Pierre?" Tante Bébé persisted.

"It isn't that I haven't wanted to," Pierre confessed. "But I might break a good football toe. Nonc Samuel says that our New Orleans method of leaving garbage cans out on our narrow banquettes is nothing short of disgraceful. He has ideas all right."

"Hope he has some tonight," Tante Bébé snapped. "I don't want to play the villain: I don't want to be a snarling wolf driving all the D'Orsay children out into the cold world."

Mama smiled at her.

Somehow Tante Bébé's cold world did not seem very miserable.

"You would make the jolliest sort of villain!" Pierre laughed, though he wondered what she meant.

Collette came in, wearing a white starched dress, made with countless tiny tucks and little ruffles. A big white bow perched like a dove on her head. Tante Bébé drew her down beside her on a satin-upholstered settee.

Mammy Margot's two youthful Negro helpers were busy in the dining room beyond the graceful Spanish arch of the hall. There was a centerpiece of pink roses, tall candles, and glittering glasses.

"Why make the confab into a party?" Tante Bébé inquired.

"Because I expect the results to be festive," Mama answered.

"You have more faith than the law gives you a right to hope for," Tante Bébé said dryly. "I talked with Monsieur La Branche yesterday, and he couldn't see a solution. Why should I have what I don't want?"

"Please, Solidelle," Mama begged. "Let's discuss things after dinner."

"Where are our grandmothers?" Collette inquired.

"Both Mère and Grand'mère are here," Pierre announced, getting to his feet to escort the two little old ladies in black silk into the parlors as they descended from their rooms above.

The children had always called their Grandmother D'Orsay Mère, a term of endearment; and they called Grandmother Jaculi Grand'mère. Tonight Mère walked very straight, her dark eyes snapping, her full skirt swirling about her slim figure. She sat down on a straight chair, her back very erect.

Grand'mère slipped into a comfortable upholstered chair, settling back plumply, her violet-blue eyes, so like Mama's, alive with contentment. Tante Evangeline Jaculi, tall and fair, in pale pink silk, came in from the dining room where she had been helping with the table decorations. She lived in one of the suites above with Grand'mère.

At the same moment Nonc Samuel appeared from the outside, bringing with him the aroma of freshly ground coffee. Meticulous as he was, Nonc Samuel carried with him always that fragrance—even when he was in evening clothes with pearl studs in his shirt and a gardenia in his buttonhole. Any time of the day or night that a fresh shipment of coffee came in at the wharves, Nonc Samuel would be seen hurrying to his combined offices and laboratory where he insisted that samples be roasted immediately. Then he made a pot of coffee and tasted the excellent drip for body and flavor. Pierre often accompanied him and had become quite a connoisseur of coffee himself. Sometimes Nonc Samuel carried a small package of a particularly fine mixture in his pocket to give to a friend.

He was a large, broad man, jolly by nature. He greeted the ladies and winked at Pierre as though they shared some intimate secret.

Then Papa came in, bringing Monsieur Gustav La Branche, now formally dressed in evening clothes.

Pierre noticed how excited his father looked as he kissed Mama. Papa was a handsome, slim man with small bones. His fresh, shaven face was distinguished by fine, dark eyes, a high-bridged nose, and a small black mustache.

Monsieur La Branche had a much wider face which once might have been framed by fair hair. He wore gold-rimmed glasses with heavy lenses. He had a ready smile and great politeness, and there was a very solid look about him.

Mammy Margot's dinner was so excellent that everybody talked about the cooking all through the meal—the Creole gumbo, the fried chicken, the perfect vegetables from the French Market, the green salad tossed together just enough to wilt the lettuce, and the mellow ice cream surrounded by a meringue as good as any Antoine ever made! A perfect dinner! But was it the prelude to a perfect evening? Papa's face looked stiff with the attempt to keep smiling.

After dinner the members of the family gathered in a semicircle in front of the fireplace in the back parlor; and Monsieur La Branche waited until everybody was comfortably seated before he flipped his coat-tails about and took off his glasses, tapping them against a full lower lip. His smile was almost benign.

"The situation in which the family finds itself," he announced, "I shall attempt to present so clearly that even the children will understand."

"If you please." Papa nodded, looking around the semicircle to assure himself that everybody was present—Mama beside him, then Pierre and Collette, then the grandmothers, then Nonc, and the two maiden aunts, Tante Bébé and Tante Evangeline.

"If you will not be bored," Monsieur La Branche continued cheerfully, "we shall start out with the demise of that fine old gentleman known to all of you as Grandpère D'Orsay, rest his soul!"

Pierre and Collette looked at each other with understanding. If it had to do with Grandpère, it was bound to be exciting.

"Nobody will be bored," Mère said with spirit. "I believe it was his death that started all the trouble."

Monsieur La Branche coughed, and Tante Bébé giggled.

"I would recall Grandpère D'Orsay to you all: a fine, tall

old man with penetrating brown eyes, a beautifully waxed mustache of snowy white, and a wide chin with a cleft in it. He himself used to say, 'Double chin, double trouble.' Even at ninety-seven he was a whimsical old man."

"Whimsical is a good word for him," Mère agreed. "He abounded in teasing."

"He was, nevertheless, stable," Monsieur La Branche affirmed, "and he had a very definite code. He told me once that he thought a gentleman should provide for his family even if he had to *work* with his own hands. Early in his married life he established a trust fund for his beloved wife." Monsieur La Branche bowed to Mère. "The rest of his property was left to his children. The will that I probated for you D'Orsays when Grandpère D'Orsay died was the first one he had drawn up when his daughter, Solidelle, was a fairly grown woman and his son was still pretty much of a boy. I believe you are all well aware of the fact that Solidelle is ten years older than her brother, Pierre, Senior."

"Why bring that up?" Tante Bébé inquired with a smile.

"Because," Monsieur La Branche explained carefully, "at the time the will was drawn up, Grandpère's most valuable property, the plantation Live Oaks, was left to the *elder* child, since the younger could not have been held responsible for some time. The younger child, however, was provided for with a gift of bank stock."

"That was Papa!" Collette squealed.

Monsieur La Branche beamed upon Collette.

"Exactly!" he said, then grew sober. "That bank stock

is now valueless since the bank failure. Absolutely worthless!"

A sigh went around the semicircle.

"The family is much poorer, but it is not impoverished," the lawyer continued hurriedly. "The Royal Street house, which Grandpère D'Orsay's father built and in which we are gathered this evening, was deeded to his son at the time of the son's marriage. It will someday be the home of Pierre, Junior, because it must always remain in the family."

Gratitude and wonder flooded over Pierre. Why, this was *his* house!

"There is no law to keep me from selling this house," Papa said sharply.

Pierre held his breath, waiting for the lawyer's answer.

"No law," Monsieur La Branche decided. "But tradition is sometimes stronger than law. A fine tradition demands that the house remain in the D'Orsay family." Pierre's head bobbed up and down in agreement, and the lawyer continued, "Shall we forget the Royal Street house for a few moments? At the time his son was born, Grandpère D'Orsay gave him a christening gift."

"What was it?" Nonc inquired, hoping to break the tension. "A rattle?"

"It was a piece of property," the lawyer specified. "It was known as the Orleans house, thought by many to be the home in which Napoleon Bonaparte was to be entertained."

"Now, now!" Nonc Samuel waggled a finger. "Let's not drag in the plot to bring Napoleon over to New Orleans. Let's stick to the situation in hand."

"I am sticking to it, sir," Monsieur La Branche snapped. "That makes *two* houses in this D'Orsay family, this Royal Street house and the Orleans house."

"Should they be properly mentioned in the same breath?" Nonc inquired, trying to make at least the children smile. "Isn't the Orleans house a shabby old building?"

"It may look that way to you." The lawyer wiped his face with a large, snowy handkerchief.

"It *is* that way, isn't it?" Nonc persisted.

"Yes—and no," replied Monsieur La Branche with dignity. "The location is a very fine one, right off Pirate's Alley, you know. Or rather, on the continuation of Pirate's Alley, for Pirate's Alley becomes Orleans Street as it crosses Royal; or if you put it the other way about, Orleans Street becomes Pirate's Alley after crossing Royal Street."

Now everybody was laughing.

"The income from that property, as I remember," Papa put in, "was a mere pittance."

"That is a matter of viewpoint," Monsieur La Branche declared. "The old baker who ran the pastry shop made a very good living out of it in his lifetime. There is a demand for a pastry shop in that neighborhood, but the baker died last year and I haven't been able to find another renter. If that pastry shop could be opened again . . ." He let his voice die down but looked significantly at Papa. Then he added softly, "We might not have to think of selling."

"A pastry shop!" Collette shouted gleefully. "Oh, Papa, do we really own a pastry shop?"

"I think it would be fun to work in a pastry shop. I'll help, Papa," Pierre offered.

"Please listen, everybody!" Tante Bébé jumped to her feet. "Enough of this nonsense! Surely Monsieur La Branche is not suggesting that my brother run a pastry shop. That is too, *too* absurd! Since the present income from the Orleans Street house could never take care of the upkeep of the Royal Street house, I have a proposition to make. My own investments are intact, and I have plenty for the rest of my life. What I propose is that my brother accept Live Oaks from me as a gift. I'd be relieved to get rid of the responsibility. Anyway, we are all sure that there must have been a later will giving it to him."

"There *was* a second will," Monsieur La Branche acknowledged. "It was drawn up in my office and properly witnessed."

Now Papa was on his feet.

"We've been through this before, and we gave up looking for that will ten years ago," he said wearily. "If you can't produce it, don't talk about it!"

"I wish I knew where it is," said the lawyer soothingly. "Grandpère D'Orsay carried his second will about with him for the sole purpose, he said, of adding small gifts from time to time. I know that he never made any change in the original division—Live Oaks to his son and funds in trust for his daughter—but he was forever recalling some old servitor who had done him a good turn. The last entry I saw was the gift of some baskets to the Praline Man who sells candy in front of the Cathedral. Just a week before he died, I chided him about his carelessness. I said, 'Monsieur D'Orsay, I do wish you'd leave that will in the office. Suppose you lose it, or misplace it, or suppose you die without remembering to tell anyone where it is. What would happen then?' "

Papa showed not the slightest interest in the story, but Monsieur La Branche went right on. " 'Well, what would happen?' he asked me in turn; and I tell you his bright eyes were sparkling and his little white mustache kept twitching.

" 'Solidelle,' I told him, 'would have to run the plantation, and your son would have to make a living out of the Orleans Street property which has some rentals and a pastry shop. If something unforeseen happens, do you expect your son to turn shop-keeper?' Oh, I remember every word I said then."

"What did he say to that?" Papa asked impatiently.

"He didn't seem to think it such a bad idea," Monsieur La Branche acknowledged ruefully. "He laughed. You see, I have no doubt that he felt that if the will had to be found, someone"—and here he looked squarely at Collette and Pierre—"someone would find it."

Pierre happened to glance at Mère and he wondered at the amused twinkle in her eye.

"Of all the silliness!" Tante Bébé cried. "Take my offer, and you won't have to run a pastry shop."

"I do not accept your gift, kind though it is, and I have no intention of running a pastry shop," said Papa, stiffly, and Pierre's heart sank at the finality of his tone.

CHAPTER 3

The Christening Gift

Pierre awoke the next morning to the sound of voices in the patio. Mère was having an early breakfast alone with Papa. Today was All Saints' Day, and Mère had probably gone out early to look over the gardens of the house. The family always decorated Grandpère D'Orsay's tomb with "home" flowers. No bought flowers for Grandpère, when they had such a wealth of blooms right on their doorstep.

But Mère wasn't talking about flowers. Pierre didn't mean to eavesdrop, but Mère's voice was anything but old and infirm and she was sitting directly underneath his galerie window. He couldn't help hearing her scold Papa, just as any mother may scold her little boy, or her big boy.

"Just because you are a D'Orsay," she was saying distinctly, "is no reason why you should not make your living the hard way. After all, riding a fine horse about a plantation and instructing the Negroes what to do may be more gentlemanly, but . . ."

"But running a pastry shop may be more manly?" Papa

inquired, amused. "Mère, I half suspect you plotted with Fate to bring this about."

"No, cheri." Mère's voice was very tender. "I am very sorry that you lost so heavily in the bank failure. But I shall be more sorry if you do not meet life with fresh courage. Set a good example to Pierre."

"How?"

"Pierre will profit by having his father work. You don't want your son to be a snob."

"Pierre's not a snob. Naturally he goes to school with the sons of the best families. He belongs with them."

"Those little aristocrats could profit by the lesson, too. It's about time they learn that a gentleman can also be a working man."

"You mean well, Mère," Papa conceded, "and I'd hate to lose the Royal Street house. But I don't know. I just don't know."

He would not commit himself to a promise.

Later, when Mammy Margot set the grillades and rice before Pierre and Collette at breakfast in the morning room, she muttered of this Monsieur La Branche who had upset the entire household with his talk of a christening gift. A christening gift indeed! As if Monsieur D'Orsay could be expected to run a pastry shop, a grand gentleman like that!

So Mammy Margot was a snob, too, Pierre reflected.

Pierre and Collette were much subdued as they rode to the cemetery on the street car named Cemeteries, their arms laden with their All Saints' Day offering.

As they got off and walked towards the whitewashed wall

of brick that enclosed the mass of tombs and monuments, Pierre said, "I've been thinking and thinking, and I wish Grandpère D'Orsay hadn't wanted Papa to run a pastry shop. I wish Mère didn't want him to either. But what can he do to keep our Royal Street house?"

"Grand'mère Jaculi says that running a pastry shop would be good for Papa," Collette reported. "She said that Papa being a Creole was a dreamer and that it took a Cajun like Mama to be practical."

"When did she say that?" Pierre inquired.

"This morning while I was in her rooms and Tante Evangeline was tying my hair bow."

"And what did Tante Evangeline say?"

"She said, 'Sh!' "

"Papa doesn't like the idea," Pierre reminded Collette, but he did not repeat the conversation he had overheard.

"That's because he doesn't think it's important," Collette said, airily. "I guess he'd run it if he knew it meant losing our home."

"It does mean losing our home," Pierre insisted. "Monsieur La Branche says this year's income must be gotten from the christening gift. Papa won't accept the plantation from Tante Bébé, and he won't even manage it for a salary because he thinks that would be like a gift, too."

"Sometimes I think it's silly to be too proud," Collette declared. "If I were Papa, I'd do anything rather than sell the Royal Street house, anything honorable, I mean. What does Papa expect to happen?"

"The only thing that would save him would be finding the will," Pierre said. "If we tried hard—"

"Maybe we could find it," Collette finished. "It's got to be someplace."

Soberly the two children made their way around an angel of white marble, so worn that the wings, like sheltering arms, drooped disconsolately.

They reached the family tomb. It was neither of marble nor of stone but of a soft brick, plastered and freshly whitewashed for All Saints' Day. The French words on the insert of marble slab had long since been obliterated, but the D'Orsays all knew it had been the words of the twenty-third psalm. "The Lord is my shepherd: I shall not want."

Atop the tomb stood a wrought iron cross, impervious to weather. It was an elaborate cross with lacy motifs of vines and lyres and delicate flowers. On the cross pieces were inscribed the dates of the births and deaths of all the D'Orsays departed this world. Brighter and clearer than all the names stood out the name of Grandpère D'Orsay who had lived to the ripe old age of ninety-seven years and seven months.

"Grandpère," Collette begged, addressing the letters glinting in the sunlight, "please give Pierre and me some idea of where you hid the will."

Pierre was shocked.

"It's sacrilegious to talk to the dead like that," he reproved his sister. "The dead are in Heaven and should not be bothered with earthly trials and tribulations."

"Grandpère wouldn't mind being bothered." Collette grinned at Pierre over her flowers. "Boost me up, will you? I'd like to lay the chrysanthemums in front of the cross."

Pierre was more thoughtful than usual as he left the cemetery with Collette.

"Where do people hide wills?" he wondered.

"I suppose it depends on what kind of people they are," Collette reasoned. "A miser would hide a will in a tin can in a wall, so he could take out the bricks from time to time and gloat over it."

"I suppose a farmer would leave a will in the pocket of an old coat when he came in from work," Pierre figured. "Grandpère was a plantation owner. He might have left the will with his accounts in his saddle pocket."

"Not bad, Pierre," Collette approved. "That's the way things might have happened. But remember that Grandpère D'Orsay must have kept his will in a safe place. If it were in just any simple place around the house, Monsieur La Branche would have found it long ago. No, I think it must be hidden in some strange place."

"If it's too strange," Pierre worried, "we might *never* find it. And I don't think Grandpère would want that."

All the way home they talked of probable and secret hiding places, and with each suggestion Pierre grew more determined to find that will.

The worries of the D'Orsay children lifted a few days later when Cousin Felix Jaculi, their good-natured, red-haired cousin from the Bayou country came to visit. His mirth was good to hear when Grand'mère Jaculi explained that the architecture of the French Quarter was Spanish and that the French Market was run by Italians. But he was most excited over his Oncle Pierre's christening gift, because to him a pastry shop was a palace of delight.

As for the missing will, he had endless ideas of where it could be found. He sat beside Grand'mère Jaculi, facing Pierre and Collette in the hack that the Negro driver rented for sightseeing. The old brown horse was more leisurely than the most dawdling tourist. There was time for everything, and everything stimulated ideas in Felix's agile mind.

At sight of the antique shops he exclaimed, "The will might be in the secret drawer of a desk. We have a desk in our house. Remember? During the French Revolution jewels were hidden in the little secret drawers behind the regular drawer that is shorter than it looks. You pull it out! But no! You find it never went to the back of the desk at all. It comes out in your hand. And there where it would have gone if it had been longer are some little secret drawers."

"Was Grandpère down in the Bayou country a few months before he died?" Collette inquired.

"No," Felix admitted. "But he might have had a desk like ours on the plantation. I guess all French desks are likely to have secret drawers."

Pierre tucked the idea of a desk with secret drawers away in the back of his mind, to be thought about more carefully later on.

A little later Felix suggested that maybe Grandpère D'Orsay had buried the will in the cobblestone-filled garden. Even Grand'mère Jaculi scoffed at that idea.

"New Orleans is not built on rock, like New York," she explained, "but over alluvial soil on piling. A will, Felix, is a piece of paper. It would go quickly to pieces in the wet soil."

"I'll think of something else," Felix promised.

He was so eager to help that the D'Orsays longed to please him. As the hack drew up at the Cabildo on Chartres Street, Collette shouted, "There's the Snowball Man! Oh, Grand'-mère, may I treat Felix to a snowball? I'm sure he has never eaten one."

"Me, I've never even seen snow, much less eaten it," Felix admitted seriously, and wondered what he had said that made his cousins laugh so heartily.

Felix stared at the large cart that the pleasant, dark-haired man trundled over to the banquette opposite the Cabildo. Even from the hack he could see the array of bottles that looked like bottles of hair tonic in a barber shop. They were of the most delectable colors, and Pierre explained that they contained syrups of the most delicious taste, lemon, orange, vanilla, strawberry, and lime.

Grand'mère gave Pierre six pennies and said, "Run over, the three of you, and have your treat. I shall rest in the hack."

The driver got down off his high seat to open the door, but Pierre and Felix were already halfway across the street, with Collette at their heels.

"Three snowballs, please," Pierre ordered importantly. "What flavor will you have, Collette?"

"I'll take strawberry," Collette decided, then hastily changed her order. "No, orange!"

"Make up your mind," Pierre advised.

"The little lady may have both," said the smiling Snowball Man.

From the huge cake of clean ice in the wagon, he shaved a paper dish full, so fine that it did indeed look like a mound of snow. Over half the mound he squirted orange syrup and over the other half strawberry. Collette began to taste hers with a wooden spoon.

"What'll you have, Felix?" Pierre inquired, with an expansive wave of his hand. "You may have any flavor or combination of flavors you wish."

Felix selected vanilla and lime, and he could not take his eyes off the bottles even as he ate.

"Me, I have an idea!" he confided to his cousins. "The will, it could have been hidden in a bottle. I've read about sailors who put important messages in bottles and threw them into the ocean and they turned up years later, safe and sound."

"Felix, you think of everything!" Collette cried. "But we wouldn't have much chance of finding a will in a bottle in the middle of some ocean."

"You do help us a lot, Felix," Pierre teased, "by thinking of the places *we won't have to look,* like under the cobblestones in the garden or in your desk in the Bayou country."

"What's the matter with the bottle?" Felix inquired with an injured air.

"Collette just told you," Pierre laughed, "and besides, the *way* people hide wills depends on the *kind* of people they are. A sailor might put a will in a bottle and seal it; or a collector of old glass might. But I never heard that Grand-père D'Orsay set any great store by bottles as bottles. He probably hid the will in some dignified manner."

Dinner in the dining room of the Royal Street house, under the sparkling crystal chandelier that flashed all the colors of a Bayou rainbow, was so elegant that Felix could hardly eat. Mammy Margot hovered over him lovingly with her best dishes. Feeding a hungry boy was a real satisfaction.

Papa, who was always courteous to everybody, no matter how worried he might be, said, "Felix, I am taking a drive tomorrow morning. Is there anything in New Orleans you'd like particularly to see?"

"Oh, yes, sir." Felix surprised everybody by speaking right up. "Me, I should like to see Margaret."

"Margaret?" Papa inquired, while the grandmothers smiled at each other in understanding.

"Yes, sir—Margaret," Felix repeated. "I have heard her

spoken of. She was once a scrub woman in the St. Charles Hotel, she who became so famous!"

"He means Margaret Haugherty," Mama explained to Papa. "You know. There's a statue of her that was bought by popular subscription. The sculptor, Alexander Doyle, did the figure."

"Oh, yes," Papa remembered.

"May I say something?" Collette inquired, happy that she had been allowed the privilege of eating dinner with the grown-ups now that Felix was visiting. "Sister Ursula said in school that at the time it was erected it was the only statue of a woman—and to a woman, in the United States."

Collette was much excited, having made her speech; but Papa's smile approved what she had said.

"We haven't been over to Margaret Place in years," he mused. "Why are you particularly interested in Margaret, Felix?"

"Because I'd like to do things like that," Felix answered. "Me, I'd like to run a dairy like she did once and maybe a bakery. I wish I might have seen Margaret trundling bread about the streets of New Orleans. Some people say she gave away half of every loaf."

"She left a fortune," Papa said. "Perhaps it was equal to half of every loaf."

"Me, I like to think she cut every loaf in half," Felix said simply.

"Anything else you'd like to see?" Papa inquired, and his small black mustache twitched. "Suppose you make three wishes in all. We'll call Margaret your Number One wish."

"Tchoupitoulas Street! I'd like to see Tchoupitoulas Street," Felix announced, "because I had such a hard time learning to spell it."

"Good!" All the family laughed.

"For my Number Three wish, I'd like to see your pastry shop, Oncle," Felix announced. "The one that was a christening gift!"

Mama got hastily to her feet, saying, "Shall we go into the parlors for coffee?" Then she turned to Pierre. "Pierre, I am sure Felix is tired. Take him with you to the garçonnière, and Toby will bring you some hot chocolate before you go to bed."

The two boys hurried across the runway to Pierre's rooms in the garçonnière, Felix breathing hard.

"Me, I said something wrong!" Felix lamented.

Pierre noticed that he started his sentences with "Me" in the Bayou fashion only when he was embarrassed or perturbed or greatly excited.

"You said nothing wrong," Pierre assured his guest. "Only Papa is much worried about business. He must be prosperous, to keep this house running."

"But a pastry shop should make one prosperous, shouldn't it?" Felix puzzled. "Margaret was so prosperous that she left a fortune. If a poor, uneducated woman could do that, think what a man like Oncle could do! Could he not do as much?"

"Of course." Pierre brought his cousin into his pleasant study and seated him in a leather-upholstered chair.

"Then why is he worried?"

"Papa doesn't want to be in business."

"Oncle? The very one to whom the pastry shop is willed? I cannot believe it. You are teasing me."

"I wish I were," said Pierre. "Papa knows nothing about business. To start a shop would upset his whole plan of life. Papa's a Creole gentleman."

"I see," Felix said. "If only he were part Cajun! He wants his family to be happy, no?"

"Certainly he wants his family to be happy!" Pierre's voice had in it a fierce, proud loyalty. "He's a Creole gentleman, I told you. And a Creole gentleman wants everybody to be happy. He has to look out for people—his Negro workers and the poor white folks . . . and . . . and everybody."

"Too bad there aren't any people in the pastry shop," Felix said with a sigh, then asked hopefully, "Or are there? No?"

"No," Pierre said listlessly. "The baker's dead."

Papa kept his word to take Felix over to Margaret Place. He had Toby get out the surrey and hitch up the team of bays. Felix sat in the front seat with Papa, and Pierre sat in the back with Collette. Although the D'Orsay children had seen the statue of the motherly woman with the knitted shawl over her shoulders, one arm protectingly about an orphan child before, they saw it anew through Felix's eyes.

Papa drove out of his way to show Felix the street with the hard-to-spell name, taking the long drive along the wharfs. From there he turned into Canal Street. Felix's number three wish was about to be realized. The children could hardly wait for the surrey to reach Orleans street. When Papa finally pulled up the team, they saw before them a large, shabby building that must have been very handsome at one time. The lower floor was, quite plainly enough, an empty pastry shop. There were two floors above, with wrought iron galeries in an oak leaf and acorn design, and a third-floor attic with dormer windows. The French windows on the second and third floors had immense green blinds that seemed to change with the sun, revealing shadows in yellow and blue. Pierre took a long, full breath.

"Is this the place, Papa?" he inquired. "Is this the christening gift?"

"This is the christening gift," said Papa.

"I like it," Collette decided.

"But, yes!" Felix exulted. "Me, I should like to trundle bread in a cart like Margaret. But you, Oncle, you can sell it from a fine shop like a gentleman and make your fortune."

Felix had said what none of the D'Orsays would have been brave enough to say. Papa recognized the small boy's sincerity and smiled at him.

Papa turned the key in the lock. The children followed him in. There were glass-enclosed counters in the front room, and in the back room there was a long stove with several ovens. Above the clean work tables stood big containers of wood and tin. Papa looked so puzzled by these surroundings that both Pierre and Collette felt sorry for him. He was certainly out of his element in a kitchen.

There was a clatter on the stairs that led down to the

street floor. The hall door opened, revealing a well of stairs. Five people stepped into the pastry shop.

"Are you the landlord, sir?" inquired a very stout, very red-cheeked man with black, snapping eyes.

Pierre noticed that the apron over the man's midriff was spotless.

"I am," Papa said. "I am Pierre D'Orsay, Senior. I believe that, to date, the estate has had charge of this property—the estate under Monsieur Gustav La Branche."

"We are your tenants," the stout man announced. "I am André Boudro, at your service. I am not a descendant of the great Boudro who cooked for Jenny Lind, but I am a very good chef. This is my wife, Annette."

The pretty, small woman in the gay print dress made a curtsy.

"Annette makes the best pastry in New Orleans," Monsieur Boudro boasted. "But neither she nor I is employed at present."

The fine-looking, tall couple in back pressed forward.

"Dr. Paul Crager and Lotta Crager, his wife," Monsieur Boudro said, with a flourish. "Dr. Crager is studying medicine at Tulane, and Lotta makes pottery. But she can also bake *petit fours*. Ah! Such little cakes! Such decorations!"

The last of the five came from behind the doctor. She was very small and fair—and frightened.

"This," Monsieur Boudro announced, with a flare of trumpets in his voice and manner, "is La Belle Marie Fortier who paints portraits." His voice trailed sadly off. "But who appreciates portraits nowadays?"

Papa's mustache had begun to twitch and his eyes to sparkle with amusement. Papa might not like or understand a pastry shop, but he liked and understood people.

"Just how far behind in your rents are you, Monsieur Boudro?" he asked gently, so gently that at first what he had said was not wholly understandable.

"Sir," Monsieur Boudro blustered. "We were paid up, all of us, until the unfortunate closing of the pastry shop following the death of the fine old baker who ran it. Even at that, we held on for another longer period, hoping. . . . I made the bread, the French bread and the *petit pains* or 'little breads'—and sometimes the brioche. The baker himself, God rest his soul, made the best brioche. Annette here did his pastries."

"Dr. Crager and Mrs. Crager?" Papa asked.

"I took care of the baker and his family—and relatives—when they were sick," Dr. Crager spoke for himself. "I was more a nurse than a doctor because I haven't my degree as yet. Lotta kept books. She is a very good typist and bookkeeper, so good that she could have gotten other jobs; but we love the old house and the pastry shop. It has been a haven for us. This spring I shall have my degree—if I can tide over until then. It will be about seven months."

"And you, Miss Fortier?" Papa asked the shy artist.

"I am a portrait painter," the girl explained in her soft voice. "But I am not a temperamental artist. I painted the pastry shop shelves. Once I designed a cake box, but it was too expensive to print. I earned my rent. We all earned our rents. And we are hoping so much, sir, that you will reopen the pastry shop and let us all go on working for you. We need the work and will give service."

All five of the tenants stared at Papa with such longing and anxiety in their faces that he could not resist them.

"What else can I do?" He spread his hands in a gesture of acceptance. "What else can I do but open this pastry shop and run it as best I can—with your help! Unless I could find another baker to rent the place to!"

"Not *that,*" they all shouted. A new baker would hire others, his relatives or friends. Besides, they pointed out, all talking at once, Monsieur D'Orsay would lose his profits.

"Very well," Papa agreed. "I shall open the shop—at once."

It would have to be at once, the children realized, or he might change his mind.

Pierre was, oh, so proud. Collette was just as proud. The needs of other people had broken down Papa's pride. That was because Pierre D'Orsay, Senior, was first, last, and always a gentleman.

"Sir," said Monsieur Boudro, with a hoarseness in his voice due to extreme emotion, "some day we will set up a statue for you—like Margaret."

"Heaven forbid!" Papa exclaimed fervently.

Bread and Brioche

PIERRE had so many new things to think about that he was lying awake in his four-poster bed in the garçonnière long before the sun came up in the morning. It was lovely just to lie and daydream. Felix had gone home to his Bayou plantation but Pierre had absorbed all his cousin's enthusiasm for the pastry shop venture. Now he was thinking about Papa's running the shop and about all the delicious cakes Monsieur Boudro would bake. He wondered if Papa would let him sell or just run errands. And he wondered what his friends would say. They'd certainly be surprised. He thought, too, about Grandpère D'Orsay; and he tried very hard to think of every desk, shelf, or closet where he might look for the missing will. But bother the will; today was pastry shop day.

The sun rose and bright rifts of golden light poured in through the shutters. Pierre tried to identify each little noise as the household woke up and set about its daily duties. There was Tante Evangeline singing as she cut roses for the breakfast table. And that was Toby running up the steps.

Toby came into the room and pushed the hassock around to the side of Pierre's bed nearest the window. He had been told, time and time again, that it was not necessary, but habit was strong with him. Ever since he was old enough to go to school, Pierre had been able to slide to the floor from the high-posted bed without the aid of the hassock.

"Time yo' was gettin' up, Mastah Pierre," Toby drawled, "eff'n yo' goin' to be in time fo' school. I gotta go to mah school too. Yo' lunch is packed."

"Go along, Toby," Pierre pleaded. "I won't go back to sleep. Honest. I've been awake hours and hours already. Who could sleep late today?"

And he jumped out of bed, suiting his words with action.

Mammy Margot had prepared the usual good school-day breakfast of grillades, hominy, brioche, and chocolate. Also there was a basket of fresh fruit on the side table.

Papa was there at the table, buttering a small *croissant,* but he did not look hungry. Mama, who usually appeared at the breakfast table in a dainty gabrielle with a lovely jacket, or sachet as she called it, over the wrapper, was dressed in severe street clothes. Pierre somehow knew that Papa would much have preferred to see Mama in her pastel, quilted silk sachet instead of a shirtwaist. The shirtwaist was tucked into a long, dark, wool skirt, and there was a wide leather belt encircling Mama's slim waist.

Usually rather sleepy and sweet-looking at breakfast, Mama wore today a very much alive look. She looked, in fact, as though never again would she say, *"J'ennui,"* which really meant, "I'm bored." Pierre had seldom seen her violet eyes sparkle so gayly, except when she was going to a Mardi Gras ball or the opera. She looked like a person about to have a very good time, only her shining dark hair with the gold in it was not curled but brushed smoothly back, pompadour style.

"Good morning, Mama," Pierre said as he slid into his place at the table. "Is there to be a parade today? Or a party?"

There were always parades in New Orleans, there were always parties. Many people called New Orleans the City that Care Forgot.

"I am going to business," Mama said, sitting very straight.

Papa said, "Bon jour, Pierre. I'm glad to see *you* about your ordinary duties." Papa was obviously regretting his impulsive promise to reopen the pastry shop immediately, and Pierre ate hastily, hoping to finish his breakfast and be out of the house before Papa could have time to announce a change of heart.

The last drop of chocolate gone, Pierre ran out into the patio where Mammy Margot was waiting to give him his lunch box. Toby, ready to leave for his school, set his books on his head, and strutted off merrily. Pierre set his books on his head, and down they tumbled. Mammy Margot laughed so hard that she shook all over. Even after she had provided a strap to hold Pierre's books neatly together, she continued to chuckle as Pierre tried and tried again to walk upright carrying the books on his head.

"If Toby can do it, why can't I?" he grumbled. "Maybe I need practice."

"Mebbe yo' does," Mammy Margot agreed. "An' mebbe yo' needs ancestry! Toby's fo'bears foh generations has ca'ied loads 'long Congo trails. They's walked straight 'n steady, all them men and women he comes from. That's w'at got Toby his fine ca'riage."

"So that's what got Toby his fine carriage," Pierre repeated.

"Yas, *sah!*" Mammy Margot said emphatically.

All mothers and grandmothers were alike in their pride, Pierre thought as he picked up his books by the strap, and swinging them, hurried out to the street and turned towards Esplanade Boulevard.

Someone called "Oo-hoo" from the front galerie of his own home, and Collette, her hair still in *couettes,* shouted, "Pierre! Come to the pastry shop after school. I'm going to be there—and Mama's going to be there—and Mère and Grand'mère."

Tante Evangeline was drawing Collette into the house, clucking about her display of *couettes* in public. People must not know that Collette's hair, fine as duck down and brown as chocolate, was straight as a string. Collette must have curls. Mammy Margot always said when Collette objected to her hair being wound tightly on the rag curlers, "God don't love ugly!"

Pierre trudged along reluctantly, wishing that he could appear at the pastry shop instead of at school.

His conjugation of French verbs was mechanical, like the slap-slap-slap of a batter spoon. But geography called for accurate knowledge, not learned by ear. When Monsieur Blont, the head master, asked for the location of the Aleutians, Pierre hesitated.

Monsieur Blont was a dapper, fair little man who always smelled of shaving lotion from Auçoin's. He tapped his silver pencil on the text in his hand while he waited.

Pierre was trying to guess. The name—Aleutians—had a lovely, soft sound, like gentle wind blowing.

"The Aleutians," Pierre recited, "are located in the South Seas."

"And how did you arrive at this conclusion?" Monsieur Blont snapped.

"I guessed, sir," Pierre admitted miserably. "The name sounded tropical."

Gaston raised his hand, shaking it, and shouted, "Pierre's only half a world away. The Aleutians are off Alaska."

Gaston Sevier looked so superior that Pierre longed for a punch at him. But he held onto his temper.

Arithmetic was no better. Pierre had a hopeless struggle with a problem about papering a room.

"Pierre," Monsieur Blont said, with elaborate sarcasm, "you may never have to paper a room, but you may sometime have to use your mind. Arithmetic is a wonderful exercise for the mind. Where *is* your mind?"

"I am sorry, sir," Pierre apologized, "but my mind is not on my work."

"His mind is on brioche," Gaston whispered.

Monsieur Blont heard. He whirled around, his coat-tails flapping up.

"Now just *what,*" he demanded, "is the foundation for a remark like that?"

"There's a foundation all right," Gaston declared, and in his voice was the ta-ta-ta of a bugle and the unfurling of a banner. "His father is opening a pastry shop on Orleans Street near Pirate's Alley."

"The French," said Monsieur Blont, severely, "are people of great imagination. Great imagination! But may I speak plainly? When those imaginations run wild, the French become great liars."

Gaston continued to grin triumphantly, and Pierre turned red with shame. He knew now that neighbors would soon hear that Pierre D'Orsay, Senior, was running a pastry shop and that Mama was "going to business," and in the eyes of his schoolmates that seemed to be a disgrace. Then into his mind flashed Mère's remark, "You don't want your son to be a snob," and proudly raising his head Pierre said clearly, "Gaston is telling no story. My father *is* opening a pastry shop on Orleans Street near Pirate's Alley. He inherited the building."

"Be more *ex*plicit, Pierre." Monsieur Blont fairly flounced. "Say, 'My father is having a pastry shop opened.' "

Pierre tried to state the facts but was waved to his seat with a peremptory gesture. He realized for the first time that there was snobbery in Monsieur Blont's school, a snobbery that had to do with prosperity as well as family. The pastry shop was an admission that the D'Orsays had to work for a living.

Nor was the Quarter quite the place to live any more; it was becoming fashionable to move into the Garden District. But for Pierre there was no house in the Garden District to compare with the house on Royal Street. That was home. He was proud of it and proud of the shop in Pirate's Alley. It didn't matter what Gaston said, or what the other boys thought.

Walking along Esplanade Boulevard after school, Pierre caught sight of two familiar figures. So Collette had not escaped the usual promenade after all. The School for Young Ladies which she attended allowed ample time for social amenities.

Today Collette was wearing an especially elaborate frock

with tiny tucks, inserts of lace, and delicate embroidery that Tante Evangeline had worked on for months. The laundress had spent two hours pressing its starchy whiteness, setting the tiny tucks and rounding out the frilly ruffles. On Collette's small hands were white gloves, and she carried a ruffled silk parasol. Mammy Margot rustled in stiff white dress and apron, and her tignon was snowy.

"So you had to parade yourself after all," Pierre teased, coming alongside the pair.

"I came to please Papa," Collette explained. "He asks what the world is coming to, with everybody in business; though I have never seen more people than today, both strolling and riding in carriages. . . . Is the French Quarter a slum, Mammy Margot?"

Collette's schoolmates, too, had been discussing the D'Orsay family, it seemed.

"A slum's a state o' mind, Miss Collette," Mammy Margot answered. "Eff'n yo' got a low mind an' no cou'age, yo' is a slum pe'son. Eff'n yo' got quality, yo' *is* quality, no mattah whar yo' lives."

She reached for Pierre's books so that he could run on, unencumbered, to the pastry shop.

He darted across Esplanade, skirting around a team of driving horses that were rearing with fear as an automobile approached. Then he rushed on along Royal Street in the direction of Canal; and it seemed to him that once he had started, he could not go fast enough. He rounded the corner at Orleans Street without even glancing over at the Cathedral Garden or Pirate's Alley.

The door to the shop was open, and everything was spankingly, sparklingly clean.

Tante Bébé and Tante Evangeline were lining the show cases with paper doilies. From the kitchen came the crusty, mellow fragrance of brioche in its final stages of baking. Mama stood in front of the stove with Monsieur Boudro and his wife, Annette, beside her. Her face was flushed but not entirely from the heat of the stove. There was about her a fine pride of accomplishment. She looked young, like Collette in long skirts.

Pierre sniffed the fragrance of vanilla and almond, and then he saw the long work tables at the far end of the kitchen. Seated at the tables, in their black silk dresses but wearing voluminous white aprons, sat the two grandmothers. Pierre went towards them slowly, unbelieving.

"Mère! Grand'mère!" he exclaimed. "What are you doing here? Does Papa know?"

They displayed their work proudly. Grand'mère Jaculi had decorated all the little cakes with frosting and nuts and fruits, and Mère D'Orsay was setting them in fluted paper cups, white and green and pale pink and lavender, so that a tray of them looked like a flower garden. Pierre had never smelled anything so good, had never seen anything so beautiful.

Then the first batch of brioche was on the work table, and André Boudro, who had drawn it from the oven, was sniffing it and blowing it a kiss with his thumb and forefinger. Pierre crowded in to look. The brioche was very brown on top, but in the edges could be seen how fine and yellow-rich the dough was. Made with rich milk and eggs and melted butter!

At this auspicious moment Papa came in from the street. A bell tinkling in the kitchen announced his coming. He greeted the two aunts briefly, and he looked in on the grandmothers with amazement written so large on his face that Mama laughed. Then, drawing him into the kitchen, she made apologies.

"Baking the first brioche and preparing the first cakes will bring the family good luck," she pleaded, "if all of us participate. Please forgive us, Papa. This work is more of a ceremony than anything else. It isn't really work: it's more like play."

André Boudro picked up one of the *croissants* made from the brioche dough. He nibbled at it, like a little rabbit nibbling at a choice bit of clover. His jaws worked and his lips. Then tears filled his eyes with the moving appreciation that one artist feels towards another artist.

"It is but the perfection!" he exclaimed, bowing to Mama. "Nobody else could make such brioche!"

Papa scowled.

"Shall I drive you home?" he asked Mama.

"Please," Mama said pleasantly. "But I should like so much to come back this evening and help with the éclairs. I really want to—if it will not make you too unhappy."

Papa said stiffly, "As you like."

Whereupon Mama kissed him and Annette clapped her hands and Monsieur Boudro whirled his towel. Pierre was given the job of unpacking paper cups for more little cakes.

In spite of the festive atmosphere, he could not help feeling sad that Papa was unhappy.

The grandmothers did not return to the pastry shop after dinner, nor did the aunts. Collette, chaperoned by Mammy Margot, was permitted a brief visit, but Pierre was allowed to stay until past midnight when all the baking was completed.

"We are now ready for customers," Papa announced in the tone of a man who has done a job that had to be done.

Even as he spoke the door burst open with a jingling of the kitchen bell, and in walked Nonc Samuel with three ladies whose corsages and perfumed dresses scented the air, and two other gentlemen in evening clothes and wearing silk hats. These guests bought samples of everything in the shop. Everybody tasted the brioche, and everybody left big orders for brioche to be delivered in the morning. Pierre realized with a flutter of excitement that the shop was practically sold out on brioche the very first hour of its existence.

After Nonc Samuel and his friends had left, André Boudro shrugged his expressive shoulders.

"They have tasted the best brioche," he declared. "Will they be satisfied with anything but the best?"

He looked significantly at Mama, and Pierre could almost see what he was thinking.

"If only," Mama said in a small, meek voice, "I might be permitted to fill these first important orders."

"I can see the handwriting on the wall," said Papa, giving in with a shrug.

"It will be handwriting on the credit side of the ledgers," prophesied André Boudro.

Pierre knew, with a troubled heart, that Mama had cleverly wedged her way into the business. Of course everybody had to help if the pastry shop were to be a success, but it was a shame that Papa could not be happy about it.

The door from the street opened again, and the little bell in back tinkled. Another customer! And this time not from within the family or the circle of friends. It was the Praline Man.

The Praline Man was very old: many people said he was over a hundred. Nobody living could remember when he had not sold pralines in front of the Cathedral of St. Louis.

He must have been a very tall man when he was young, for even now he seemed to loom over the sparkling glass counter, the bright eyes in his wrinkled face smiling at Pierre knowingly. But the moment Papa appeared behind Pierre, he stiffened. Then he grinned impudently.

"Monsieur D'Orsay running a pastry shop?" he inquired, his voice implying that the high and mighty may fall.

"We are closing," Papa said coldly. "As a matter of fact, this shop is not opened as yet. What did you want?"

"Please let me wait on him, Papa," Pierre begged. It was fun to be selling something to the old man instead of buying candies from him.

The Praline Man bought a yard-long loaf of French bread, the kind one eats with gumbo.

"Thank you, sir," Pierre said, accepting the coin from the brown, wrinkled old hand.

As the Praline Man turned to go, Papa stared at him. This old fellow in the gypsy-like garments and the basket of candies belonged somewhere in the scheme of things. Pierre looked from his father to the old man and back to his father. The old man stopped before the door to wind his shawl more tightly about his lean figure. Suddenly Pierre turned excitedly to his father and whispered, "Grandpère's will, isn't he . . . ?" He didn't have to say one word more.

"Just a moment!" Papa cried, as the Praline Man closed his fingers on the handle of the door. The old man turned slowly. Papa hesitated, cleared his throat; he had never spoken to the Praline Man before.

"Ah, my good man," he began, "are you aware that you are the last person mentioned in my father's will—a will that is at present missing? In return for some favor of the distant past, he left you a gift of baskets. Are you aware of that? And are you further aware that if we could find this will now, it would mean a great deal to us?" Papa glanced around the shop and added sorrowfully, "A great deal indeed."

The Praline Man slowly turned the handle of the door. Opening it, he said, "I am aware."

Then he went out. Whether or not he knew anything more about Grandpère or the will, Pierre and Monsieur D'Orsay couldn't tell.

The Praline Man

THE next day was Saturday, and in the evening Nonc Samuel offered to shop at the French Market for the busy D'Orsay family. He appeared in the doorway of the pastry shop after dinner, wearing brown tweeds, a soft felt hat on his head, and a jaunty walking stick in his hand.

"Everybody ready?" he shouted. "How about some coffee and doughnuts at the French Market?"

"Just the children!" said Mama, appearing in the doorway. "Pierre may have the café au lait, but Collette had best drink just the hot milk."

The three walked through Pirate's Alley and crossed the street to the park. Glancing back Pierre saw the Praline Man, who had been sitting on the Cathedral steps as usual, pick up his basket and move on in the dusk. After the masses were said for the day, few tourists loitered near the Cathedral, and the last of his candies always sold faster in the busy market streets.

"Poor old man!" Collette sympathized. "He looks so tired and lonely. I just bet he'd like to visit with us."

"He visits all day long," Pierre informed his sister. "There's hardly a minute when somebody isn't asking him where to find Antoine's or the Napoleon death mask, or the Haunted House."

"But that's not like visiting with us," Collette cried. "We're fun!"

The French Market was in plain view now. The great arcaded brick and plaster columns looked softly rosy under the night lights. From across the street the fruits and vegetables, arranged in piles and pyramids on the slanted tables, were a riot of color and form and beauty.

After crossing at St. Ann, the visitors walked rapidly past the fish market, and Nonc paused at the end of the first platform to buy Collette a bouquet of cape-jasmine.

"Lovely!" Collette breathed into it. "It helps cover up the fishy smell."

A cold drizzly wind was blowing in from the river over the fruits and vegetables. Here and there, all along the arcade, stood charcoal braziers, glowing. Frequently Nonc stopped to warm his hands.

"This *air courant*—this draught—is not good for my health," Nonc complained, hunching over in imitation of an old woman wearing a shawl. "I should have a cap that I can pull down over my ears like the one that old Praline Man wears. However, let's do this shopping up right."

He led the way into the Mexican stall where he bought the largest basket in sight. It was, in fact, the size used by truck gardeners, the dealer explained.

"Suppose we begin at the first stall and go all the way down," Nonc, in high good-humor, suggested.

Collette chose some beautiful Satsuma oranges and some kumquats with their own green foliage. Then Pierre added a few Louisiana navels that weighed over a pound apiece and several beautiful white cauliflowers because Mère liked them so much.

The Italian woman who waited on them added a bunch of parsley, some green onions, and a little bouquet of fresh thyme.

"Lagniappe!" she said with a smile, meaning that she was giving her shoppers a present.

At the next stall Nonc himself heaped in some bright red apples and Collette chose a purple eggplant. There were Italian beans too, their long, green pods adding to the beauty of the basket.

"Lagniappe!" This time a small Italian man added a bunch of soup vegetables to the already full basket.

A third stall, a fourth, a fifth, a sixth! Bananas and garlic and yams! And always more lagniappe!

By this time Nonc was very warm indeed, in spite of the breeze from the river. He actually sagged under his burden.

"May I help you, Nonc?" Pierre inquired.

"*May* you?" Nonc was puffing. "You'll *have* to help me."

They carried the basket between them across the street to the coffee shop. Shaking the raindrops off their hats, the three climbed up on the tall stools at the center counter, the counter with the mirrors and the great silver sugar bowls. Nonc passed his walking stick over to Pierre who laid it carefully in front of him at the end of the table; the basket reposed between Collette and Nonc on the floor. It was very cozy inside, listening to the rain on the roof.

An alert waiter stood at Nonc's elbow, and Nonc said, "Coffee and doughnuts for three," forgetting all about hot milk. It made Collette feel grown-up.

"There's a trick to serving French Market coffee," Nonc said. "Watch!"

The chef held two silver pots very high as he stood at the counter at the far end of the room. From the unusually long spouts came two streams of liquid, one black coffee essence, one boiling hot milk. There was foam on top of the cups when they were brought and sugary doughnuts on the plates, hot raised bread just out of the fat.

As Pierre lifted his cup, he stopped suddenly. Looking out through the glass door he saw the Praline Man. His head was down against the wind as he proffered the large, flat candies in their oil paper to the crowds coming to the coffee shop. Some bought; a stevedore took several. The rain from the eaves was now a curtain.

If only he would come in! It was warm and pleasant inside.

The stools filled up all along the counter, and so did the little tables—stevedores, farmers, opera goers, football players, visiting salesmen, tourists! Then several of Nonc's opera-going friends came in and sat at the counter.

Nonc reached down, lifted the heavy basket and set it before them. His smile was ingratiating.

"Could I interest you, Monsieurs and Mesdames," he inquired, "in some very fine fruits and vegetables? I have the most beautiful eggplant, the finest cabbages, the most luxurious parsley. Where else will you find such luxurious parsley? I sell very cheap, to lighten my load."

Pierre and Collette could not help laughing, nor could the newcomers. But a stalwart farmer who had been sitting on a stool next to Pierre, got slowly to his feet and lumbered around to where Nonc was holding forth on the merits of his produce.

"Why you sell in here?" the farmer demanded. "You gotta license?"

"I have no license, and you have no sense of humor," Nonc declared. "That makes us even."

"Even?" the farmer roared. "What do you mean—even?"

The proprietor came rushing up. The children slid off their stools, and Collette tugged at Nonc's arm.

"Please, oh, please, let's go home, Nonc Samuel," she begged.

"I'll take the basket," Pierre offered, tugging at it.

Nonc's friends, in the meantime, were trying to explain to the farmer that the basket belonged to Nonc alone, for his family.

The farmer ruffled the top of the immense basket with an experienced hand.

"All these parsleys—one family?" he scoffed.

Nonc was getting tired of the discussion; it was too absurd. He brandished his walking stick in the face of the farmer, who refused to back down. When the man grew even more belligerent, now that he had an audience, Nonc suddenly performed what looked like magic. He made a swift gesture with his right hand and drew from his walking stick a sharp, bright sword.

Pierre and Collette screeched like a cheering squad for a football team. They knew that men in the French Quarter once carried swords in their walking sticks for protection; but they had not known that Nonc had one.

The farmer and the proprietor recoiled. A waiter yelled, "Police! Police!" and started running toward the door just as it opened to admit a very wet old man.

"What's going on here?" the old man asked. Everybody stopped shouting at once and turned to look at him.

"The Praline Man!" Collette and Pierre chorused together.

He smiled at them and nodded to Nonc. All the noise began again as the farmer, the proprietor, and Nonc tried to tell the Praline Man what *was* going on. They sounded so funny—all talking together—that the children burst out laughing. The proprietor threw up his hands in amusement and went back to work. Only the farmer was still angry. The Praline Man put a friendly hand on his shoulder and explained that Nonc was not in the vegetable business. He explained that Nonc belonged to the D'Orsay family and, with an extra twinkle in his eye, added, "That family is in the business of selling pastry, in the shop on Orleans Street, just off Pirate's Alley."

Pierre reddened, and Collette felt like making a curtsy, as if she had been introduced. The farmer nodded his head understandingly, shook hands with Nonc, and went out with the Praline Man.

"Well, that was a clever advertising stunt," one of the tourists laughed.

Nonc and Pierre picked up their basket, Collette opened the door for them, and everybody shouted good night as they left. Outside the coffee shop the Praline Man was still standing in the rain. Nonc beckoned to him.

"We must thank you," he said, "for your service. How did you happen to be here, just when we needed you?"

"Always," said the Praline Man, "I walk around in the Quarter until I have sold my basketful. Here near the *Morning Call* people come and go twenty-four hours."

"That's no reason for an old man like you to come and go twenty-four hours a day," Nonc Samuel chided, reaching into his pocket. "How many pralines have you left?" he asked.

"Oh, no, sir!" The Praline Man drew back proudly. "There are very few; I am going home now."

Nonc respected the Praline Man's pride.

"What's your name?" he asked abruptly.

"Josef," the old man answered. "Josef Garavalia. Monsieur D'Orsay always called me Josef, my given name."

"Monsieur D'Orsay?" Nonc asked. "You do not mean Pierre D'Orsay, Senior, the father of these children?"

"No, sir, I do not!" He spoke with a hint of contempt. "I mean the grand old gentleman you call Grandpère D'Orsay."

It was plain to all three D'Orsays that Josef considered Papa a pampered aristocrat, scarcely worthy of being the son of Grandpère D'Orsay.

The rain poured down so hard now that it spattered up about their feet as they huddled under the wide eaves of the Coffee Shop. Nonc finally managed to signal a cab.

"Get in!" Nonc ordered Josef after he had seated the children.

"It is only a short way, over on St. Philip (he pronounced it Fee-leep)," he began, but this time Nonc Samuel was firm.

The Praline Man sat stiffly beside Nonc Samuel, facing Collette and Pierre, his basket on his lap.

"I have an idea!" Collette announced as the cab began to move into the narrow rue Dumaine. "Couldn't we sell pralines at the pastry shop? Then Josef wouldn't have to sit all day on the Cathedral steps."

"But, that is my *life!*" Josef cried.

"I have it!" Pierre shouted. "Josef could bring his left-over pralines to us every day after sundown. Many people come into the shop when they smell the bread at midnight, after the opera."

"That," decided Nonc, "is a sane suggestion that you cannot ignore, Josef."

The very old man regarded the children with his bright, burning eyes.

"It is like your Grandpère D'Orsay being alive again," he said.

The last that the D'Orsays saw of the Praline Man was the sight of his tall, bent figure pushing open a shabby, wooden door into a cavernous courtyard, black as the rainy night.

"Queer old duck!" Nonc remarked, lifting his long legs over the basket.

"Do you suppose he knows a lot about Grandpère?" Collette inquired.

"He thinks he does," Nonc said shortly.

"I guess he wants his baskets," Pierre mused. "They must be very special baskets, to be left in a will."

Nonc yawned. Collette yawned. Pierre yawned.

CHAPTER 6

The Missing Desk

SUNDAY breakfast, still as elaborate as usual, was served in the D'Orsay household after the early mass which the grown-ups attended. There were grillades (rounds of veal stewed down in rich brown gravy), snowy hominy, *petits pains* or "little breads" with marmalade and pure coffee essence, to be served with the pitchers of hot milk for café au lait. A basket of fruit from the Saturday night marketing graced the side table.

Pierre and Collette enjoyed their hot chocolate and munched the crisp crescents spread with sweet butter. Right after breakfast, Collette went off to the children's mass; but Pierre lingered, for he attended the longer service at eleven.

Nonc Samuel poured himself a cup of coffee and settled down beside Pierre to drink it.

"If you see Josef at church," he suggested, "I think it would be well to remind him to leave some of his pralines at the shop this evening."

"I'll tell him," Pierre promised. "And I'll tell you what he says."

"By the way, Pierre," Nonc said, "your father is somewhat troubled because business isn't going as well as he would like. Having had no experience in trade, he expects profits the very first week. He's to talk things over with Monsieur Boudro. You might stop in from church and walk home with him."

"I will," Pierre promised again. "And I'll try to cheer him up."

By the time Pierre reached the Cathedral, the bells were chiming. Usually the Praline Man sat with his basket of flat, nut candies, each one done up in a piece of oil paper, on the Cathedral steps, waiting for the church-going tourists to come out. He was not there today, and Pierre missed him. He was part and parcel of Saint Louis' and he even seemed old like the Cathedral, too. The façade at which Pierre squinted in the sunlight, with its tall central spire and twin lateral spires, was only fifty years old. The Praline Man was twice that. His head must be as full of memories as his face was full of wrinkles. But just how much would he tell?

Pierre stepped softly into the church with its high vaulted walls. The marble floor felt cold after the warm sun, and the richly dark benches were cool to the touch. He settled into his pew, his eyes roving from the stained glass windows and mural paintings to the candles burning in red glass near the altar. Pierre's eyes lifted to the painting by the great Humbrecht above the altar, representing the proclamation of the Ninth Crusade by Louis XIV of France. How elegant were the King's robes, how royal his bearing, how beautiful his hands! This was the Louis for whom the Cathedral had been built. Yet the priest in his sermon was saying that the humble serve as well. Could a man serve by selling pralines or bread? Of course.

The altar candles burned gold and white as Pierre murmured his responses. Then two rows in front of him he discovered the Praline Man. He was slow at kneeling, and his rising was plainly laborious.

After the mass he made his way slowly into the sunlight where Pierre awaited him.

"Bon jour, Josef," Pierre greeted the old man. "You haven't forgotten last night, I hope. We are expecting you to bring your pralines to the shop, remember!"

"I should prefer to ask your father's permission first," the Praline Man said, hesitantly.

"Then walk over with me now," Pierre suggested. "He is in the shop. Please."

Josef nodded assent, and they turned the corner of the building into Pirate's Alley.

"You must have known Grandpère D'Orsay well," Pierre began conversationally as they walked past the Cathedral Garden.

"I did," Josef revealed. "I drove his carriage for many years. That was after I left the pirates."

Pierre could not believe he had heard aright.

"Pirates did you say?"

"Yes. Pirates." Josef smiled to himself.

Pierre's heart was beating faster, and it was not because he had to take such long steps either.

"Lafitte could not have done without my father and me,"

the Praline Man boasted. "Jean became the leading smith of his time, but it was my father who taught him to shoe a horse. My father became his most trusted lieutenant. No, Jean Lafitte, the greatest of all pirates, could not have done without Dominique You or my father or me—*or a certain other one.* I was but your age at the time. Someday I will show you the small sword, forged in Lafitte's blacksmith shop, with which I was forced to defend myself."

Josef talked on of his own prowess, but Pierre's thoughts were on that *certain other one* who had played a part in this scheme of things. That must have been his own Grandpère D'Orsay!

Papa was alone in the shop when they arrived.

"I have brought Josef with me," Pierre announced, "because he wants to be sure that he is welcome to leave his pralines here. . . . And he knows some exciting things about Grandpère D'Orsay."

"What sort of things?" Papa inquired, facing the newcomers from behind the counter.

"About his being mixed up with the pirates," Pierre specified.

"I think he knows," the Praline Man blazed. "Surely he must have been told that Monsieur, young as he was, was with us on the plot to rescue Napoleon from Elba—later from Saint Helena." Josef's eyes seemed to be looking back into the past. His voice was almost reverent with the memory, as he continued. "There were Girard, Captain Boussière, and Béluche, and I was their cabin boy. What plans were made in my father's house! Had we succeeded, we'd have had the emperor over here in New Orleans where he would have been happy—where he'd have lived to a ripe old age. . . ." He seemed to return to the present and spoke directly to Papa, "Can you realize, sir, how it broke our hearts, the news of Napoleon's death, coming as it did on the eve the *Seraphine* was to sail?"

"It was a dangerous plot," Papa snapped. "It might have cost Grandpère D'Orsay his hot young head! Mère would never permit any mention of those days; not of that affair or of the piracy either." Even now Papa wished the subject closed.

The Praline Man simply lowered his voice, his eyes still on Monsieur D'Orsay, but he was addressing Pierre. "Grandpère D'Orsay wasn't afraid. He even had a beautiful desk for the Emperor. . . . But when the plot blew up, he had to get rid of it mighty quickly. We all went into hiding, with the law right after us."

"What became of the desk?" Pierre asked.

The Praline Man shrugged.

"That is a question I should like to be able to answer," he admitted. "One thing I do know: it was not destroyed. *It is somewhere at this very minute.*"

"If your memory serves you right," Papa put in.

"This I know. It was one of the last times that I took the old gentleman driving. He was not so well as he had been, and he said to me, 'Josef, we are growing old. . . . At least I have the desk as a souvenir of those great days.' "

The Praline Man spoke sadly, and Papa did not doubt his word.

"You did not question him as to the whereabouts of the desk?" Papa inquired.

"Naturally not, sir."

"I can't understand why Collette and I never knew about the desk, Papa," Pierre puzzled.

"I never knew about the desk myself until this moment," Papa acknowledged. "If Mère knows about it, she has locked it away in her memories. I never heard her mention it."

Then the Praline Man amazed both Papa and Pierre by announcing suddenly, "I, too, have a souvenir of those great days."

"What is it?" Pierre shouted.

"I shall be glad to show it to the grandson of Monsieur D'Orsay if he will come with me," Josef offered. "It is in my home."

"May I go, Papa?" Pierre begged excitedly.

"Go ahead." Papa gave his ready consent. "I want my own curiosity to be satisfied, too. Be home in time for dinner."

All the way to St. Philip Street Pierre kept up a continual chatter, slowing his steps to match the old man's weary stride. When they reached the faded green gate in the wall of shabby plaster, the Praline Man pushed through with Pierre at his heels.

Now they were in a large tenement court with many clotheslines looped across the wooden runways and galeries.

Rickety black stairs rose from the blackened brick floor to the second and third stories. The courtyard was no patio, though two scraggly banana palms waved torn, corded silk leaves, and a few little ferns struggled through the moist bricks of the walls.

"Come right along," the Praline Man called back.

Pierre followed him up a dark flight of steps, not much wider than the rungs of a ladder. The railing was narrow and wobbly, of unpainted, decaying wood.

The next flight was even shakier, and there were cracks between the boards through which Pierre could see the brick floor far down. His knees were shaking as his hand groped for a rail. Only his desire to know more urged him on.

When the Praline Man unlocked his door, Pierre drew a long breath of relief. The kitchen, into which they stepped from the hall, was scrubbed looking. Strangely enough, there was no stove, only a table, two chairs, and a dish cupboard.

"I had a stove once," the Praline Man answered Pierre's unspoken question. "But Mama Rossini has twelve children and no stove that is any good. I lent her my stove. Forever."

The front room was immense and bare looking. Once it must have been a salon, for there was still a rosette in the ceiling from which had doubtless hung a crystal chandelier. Now a wire dangled there, an unshaded electric light bulb at the end.

Under the bulb stood a table on which had been placed a large slab of grayish, mottled marble. It was shiny clean, ready to receive the next batch of pralines.

A brazier filled with charcoal stood beside it, and there were wooden containers of cracked pecans, casks of pure cane sugar, and great bottles of flavoring, the secret of Josef's pralines.

"He'p yourself," the host invited, indicating the crisp nuts. "Put some in your pocket. Don't be stingy with yourself. I have plenty."

Pierre tasted a few perfect halves; they were of a rich and fine flavor. He accepted a praline from the wide, flat basket so familiar to tourists. Would Grandpère's baskets be like this one?

"You're very generous," Pierre offered. "Mammy Margot always says, 'Keep yo' hands *open,* 'cause no good can come into a *shet* hand.' According to that, you ought to prosper."

"I do well enough," Josef chuckled. "Queer business for a pirate to be in. Lafitte became a blacksmith, and I became a candy maker. Your grandfather . . . you knew about him, of course."

Pierre was eager to hear more about Grandpère D'Orsay but the Praline Man was busy at his brazier, and the subject of pirates seemed closed.

"You see what I have for dinner, Pierre? I hope you did not think I dine on pralines. Soup is my dish, gumbo. Behold!" Josef lifted an iron kettle from a cask and set it beside the brazier until he should get the charcoal going. "Join me?"

"Thank you, but I have to go home to dinner."

Pierre hesitated a moment, wondering if Josef had forgotten why he had come home with him. With a little embarrassment he said, "You were to tell me about your souvenir, you know. Has it anything to do with the desk?"

"Ah, yes, indeed," Josef reminded himself as he straightened up. *"Everything.* Come with me."

Off the salon there was a small room with an iron bed in it. The blankets on it were worn but clean. There was a marble-topped washstand with bowl, pitcher, towels, and a bar of pink soap. The Praline Man picked up the bar, sniffed it, and passed it to Pierre to sniff.

"Roses!" he exclaimed. "From Mrs. Rossini for my birthday."

There were two simply framed pictures on the wall, a communion certificate for one Josef Francis Garavalia, and a photograph of a pretty, dark-haired woman with two small children.

"My family," he said gently. "I lost them with yellow fever."

Pierre's throat felt tight.

"And *now!"* Pierre followed his every movement as the Praline Man took the communion certificate from the wall. He removed the small nails that held the wooden back in place. Between the wooden back and the certificate he revealed a pen and ink sketch, yellow and faded with age, which he handed to Pierre.

"The desk," he said simply. Then he added, with a note of triumph in his voice, "Monsieur D'Orsay always said that a desk like that was a proper place for valuables."

Pierre's hands shook with excitement.

"It looks like a fancy, marble-topped highboy," he cried.

The Praline Man was looking at the sketch over Pierre's

shoulder. His long finger pointed. "That upper front panel pulls down to make a writing surface. There are two identical drawers above it. The wood is curly maple."

"What are all those little diamonds around the whole front of the desk?" Pierre inquired.

"Wood inlays for decoration," the Praline Man explained. "The lower part opens like a door for stationery and books."

"Wood inlays for decoration!" Pierre could not take his eyes off the complicated workmanship. "What a lot of work! No wonder Grandpère bought the desk. It's beautiful!"

Then he faced about and looked straight up at the Praline Man.

"But how did you get this picture?" he asked.

"I hauled the desk from the ship on which it arrived to the warehouse," the Praline Man explained. "Your Grandpère D'Orsay gave me this picture, which he had received from the cabinet maker. It was sent for the purpose of identifying the desk. When he had made certain that the desk was the right one, Monsieur D'Orsay handed the picture back to me. 'Here, Josef,' he said, 'maybe you'd like to keep this for a souvenir.' And I kept it."

"You must value it very highly," Pierre said, ashamed of his doubts as to how the Praline Man had come into possession of it.

"I do indeed." The old man appeared to be musing. "For many years I had dreams of really seeing the desk again. Once your Grandpère D'Orsay hinted that if I were ever in need, the picture might help me out."

"How?" Pierre inquired. "How, sir?"

"Because it is the only clue to finding the desk," Josef answered, "and there will be people who will want it. Once the search for it would have been a gay challenge to me. Now I am too old to make the effort."

"*I* think it is a gay challenge," Pierre declared.

"Of course," the bright old eyes caressed the very young man. "Finding the desk might make a great deal of difference in your life. Take the picture with you. It is yours! Don't stand staring at me like that, as though I were giving you a fortune. Take the picture, and welcome!"

Pierre was more certain than ever that the missing will was in a desk, and maybe this was the desk. He hurried home, the picture slipped carefully into his blouse. The relatives and friends who always stopped in at D'Orsays' after Mass to visit for an hour or so had departed, and dinner was ready to be served.

Several guests remained for dinner, and Pierre had no

chance to talk with his father though he was aware of the current between them: Papa wanting to know, he wanting to confide. In the afternoon other callers began to fill the house, and by supper the usual group was there with everybody enjoying the buffet meal—cold meats, salads, and *petit-fours*. Everyone but Pierre, that is, who was bursting with impatience to impart his news to Papa! He was so fidgety that his mother finally rebuked him, and reminding him that tomorrow was a school day, she sent him off earlier than was necessary.

"Good night, Papa," Pierre managed to say when his father turned from one group of friends to visit with another.

"Good night, cheri."

Pierre walked disconsolately down the stairs to the patio and up the short runway to the garçonnière. He was in his study taking off his coat when he heard familiar steps, and his father knocked hastily before stepping into the room.

"I thought I'd never get away," he said. "Tell me, what did you learn?"

Dramatically Pierre drew the sketch from his blouse and passed it to his father.

"Look at that!" he cried. "It is the desk!"

Papa scrutinized the picture carefully.

"Your Grandpère D'Orsay never had a desk like that," he said. "If he did, I have never seen it."

"But he might have hidden it," Pierre said. "Since it was to be for Napoleon, he had to hide it."

"But where?" Papa groaned.

CHAPTER 7

Plantation Christmas

THE desk that Grandpère D'Orsay had bought for the exiled Emperor was as real to Pierre as any piece of furniture in his study. He saw it as clearly as though it stood in front of him. In imagination he touched the cool marble top. Carefully he let down the panel to make a writing surface. He opened the two drawers above, to take out writing material, crested stationery and envelopes, and a gold pen. Often, in tender appreciation, he ran his hands over the inlaid, diamond-shaped mosaics that framed the front of the desk.

The gift for Napoleon! Where could it be? Even if it were discovered, would the will be found in it? The Praline Man had said that Grandpère D'Orsay had told him it was a proper place for valuables. Surely a will was a valuable.

Pierre sighed and with an effort pushed the thought of the desk, the will, and Grandpère D'Orsay from his mind. He was sitting at his own desk in the garçonnière, with his school work piled in front of him. Term examinations were scheduled before Christmas vacation, and he was still determined to win the scholarship.

He worked quietly and diligently for the next few hours, then closed his books with a bang. Finished for the day; and he still had time to run down to the pastry shop before dinner. Mammy Margot was out with Collette; he had to go alone.

Pierre ran through Pirate's Alley and gave a shout of greeting when he came in sight of the beautiful, swinging sign in front of the shop. Marie Fortier had designed it in the shape of a bold pirate. Gold letters shaped from "pieces of eight" formed the spelling—PIRATE PASTRY SHOP. Black letters below invited customers to "Come through Pirate's Alley." Anyone coming through Pirate's Alley could not help seeing the sign.

Too bad, Pierre thought, that there were only paper pirates nowadays. Just one pirate hold of treasure and the D'Orsays would have all the money they could use!

Monsieur Boudro boomed out a jolly hello when he saw Pierre.

"Is that Pierre?" Marie Fortier's voice called from the back room. "Just in time to help assemble the new cake boxes," she said when he appeared. "Do you like them, Pierre?"

On the tables were piles of collapsed boxes which Marie was busily setting up into proper shape. Pierre looked them over eagerly.

"They're beautiful," he exclaimed delightedly. Dainty, penciled pirates decorated the boxes for the little cakes, while the boxes for brioche boasted a black silhouette with rakish hat and boots and a wicked cutlass.

"But I'll bet no pirate ever looked like that." Pierre pointed to the funny fat pirates with flowing mustaches on the children's birthday cake boxes.

"Maybe not," Marie agreed, "but I couldn't make them all alike."

"What gave you the idea for those wicked-looking fellows on the brioche boxes?" Pierre asked as he finished putting one together.

"That is something I want to show you. I found it in my room when I first moved in. You keep working while I get it."

Marie was back in no time, and in her hand she held a wooden pirate figure, about six inches high but only two inches thick. It looked as if it had been carved out of a board and then had the face and clothes painted on.

"And this bold fellow," Marie laughed, "was hiding in a corner of the top shelf of my closet. He looked at least fifty years old; all faded beyond recognition. But I touched him up with my paints."

"Now he looks ready to scuttle a ship," Pierre said as he examined the figure.

"I wonder if this was a pirate pastry shop fifty years ago," Marie mused.

"My grandfather was a pirate, you know," Pierre told her. "And this building belonged to . . ." He stopped suddenly as a thought came to him. Quickly he turned to Marie: "Marie, did you find anything else in that closet?"

"Why, no, Pierre. What sort of thing do you mean?"

"Envelopes or papers; like a will or something. You see

Grandpère D'Orsay owned this building, and he kept his last will someplace, and your finding the pirate in your studio made me think that maybe he kept some of his things there; but I guess if you never found anything and it was so long ago . . ." Pierre had to stop for breath.

"I'm quite sure there's no will in my place, but I can make a little search if you like." Marie so wanted to please him.

"May I help you search?" he asked eagerly.

"Of course you may. But let's finish the boxes first."

Pierre began setting up boxes so quickly he had no time to say another word.

"Well, well," a voice interrupted the silence. It was Papa. "Didn't expect to find you here now, Pierre. Do you know what time it is?"

"Hello, Papa. Look at the boxes, and look at this wooden pirate that Marie found in her closet. We're going to look around and maybe we'll find the missing will hidden up there too."

"This is all very nice indeed." Papa approved the boxes and congratulated Marie. "But I don't believe Miss Fortier is hiding our missing will and we'd best get home as fast as we can or we'll be late for dinner."

Pierre was disappointed but he knew that Papa was very strict about being on time for dinner and there was no use in asking to stay longer. The search would have to be postponed. He wanted to take the pirate figure home to show Collette, but Papa said that Marie deserved to keep it for her excellent work with the sign and boxes.

At dinner the talk was all about Grandpère D'Orsay and

pirates. Afterwards the family gathered around the coal fire burning cozily in the grate. The group wasn't as large as usual because both aunts were at the plantation getting ready for the Christmas holidays and Nonc was away on business.

"The really lucrative trade," Papa observed, "is the tourist trade. If we could get the tourists to take an interest in our shop, business might improve tremendously."

"People expect stories about everything in the Quarter," Mama mused. "But almost everybody is satisfied with something simple. The Court of the Two Sisters is patronized largely because of the two sisters who once ran a little sewing shop there. The guests savor the story along with the good food."

"There are plenty of exciting stories though," Papa recalled. "Lafitte's Blacksmith Shop, as a tavern, is a rendezvous for New Orleaneans and strangers alike, because of the fact that Jean Lafitte once ran a smithy there. The old Absinthe House, with its secret half-story, stimulates people's imaginations because here the smuggled goods of pirates were concealed—before Jean Lafitte became patriotic and helped Andrew Jackson."

A secret half-story! It rang a bell in Pierre's imagination. If a half-story of a house could be kept secret for years, could not a secret hiding place for a will be in some obvious place?

Mama was saying, "Lafitte did run the smithy and he did store plunder in the old Absinthe House; but Napoleon never saw the Napoleon house. Yet tourists visit the place just because he *might have lived* there if he had been rescued from his island prison and *if* he had not died on the eve of his rescue. Then, of course, there's the Haunted House with its really true story of the woman who tortured her slaves and that awful tale of the revenge wrought upon the young sheik who stole his brother's harem."

"Nearly every house in the Quarter has a story," Pierre remarked. "Why should the pastry shop be the only place without a story?"

"We could make up a story," Collette suggested just as Mammy Margot came in and whisked her off to bed.

It was Mère who surprised them with what Pierre thought was a more important story than any of the others.

"Perhaps," she told them in her gentle voice, "the Orleans house had more to do with Napoleon than people think. There is some doubt, you know, that the home of Monsieur Girard was the one intended for the exiled Emperor. Actually three houses were considered: one was two doors from the Girard house, but across the street, on *rue* Chartres, and the other I seem to remember was on Orleans Street, the site of our own Pirate Pastry Shop."

"Wonderful!" Pierre shouted and jumped out of his chair in excitement. The others were too astonished to hear Mère herself speak of the plot to say a word. If she didn't think it would help business at the pastry shop, Papa was sure she never would have spoken.

Mère smiled back at their astonished faces and went on to say that, regardless of Napoleon, she believed that the Orleans house was very important to Grandpère. Now that she thought of it, she remembered that Grandpère often went off to a retreat of his own, where he could be alone to think things through, and there was every reason to believe that the Orleans Street house harbored his retreat.

"Do you think Grandpère made that wooden pirate?" Pierre asked.

"I wouldn't be surprised." Mère smiled. "You'll find out more about your grandfather when you come to the plantation for Christmas."

"And now to bed, young man," Papa interposed.

Pierre went off, planning his holiday on the plantation and resolving to look for all the clues possible.

The next day the grandmothers went away to the plantation to rest for a few days before Christmas festivities.

The D'Orsay family, taking Mammy Margot with them, did not arrive at Live Oaks until Christmas Eve.

The whole heavens were sparkling with bright stars when Papa turned the two fine bays that drew the surrey into the great avenue of live oaks that led up to the plantation house. It was this archway of trees that had given the plantation its name, Live Oaks.

Tante Bébé came running to meet the carriage. She wore a beautiful red velvet dinner frock and sparkling rings on her expressive hands.

"Welcome!" she cried. "Oh, we shall have the merriest of Christmases!"

A stalwart colored man stepped up to take the bridle of the near horse.

"Evenin', Mistah D'Orsay," he said. "Mighty fine to see yo', suh."

Other Negroes crowded up, all with gleaming, white-toothed smiles, and Papa said, "Excuse me, please," to his family and went off with them towards their cabins.

Tante Bébé said, "They've missed him like children. I'm no good at running a plantation. I suppose I should stay right here, but I'm so used to being in town in the winter. And what I don't know about cotton and sugar-cane would fill a very large book. . . . Oh, it's so good to see you all."

Collette ran ahead as Mammy Margot took Mama's small bag; and together she and Pierre burst in through the open door of the great hall where a giant cedar tree glittered with tinsel and baubles. The tinsel was silver rain and the baubles were jewels more precious than any the Baratarian pirates had ever found in treasure chests. Everywhere there were Christmas greens; the staircase was entwined with smilax and ground-pine.

The rooms in the Royal Street house had always seemed large even to the D'Orsays themselves—until they visited the plantation house. Here the rooms were of monumental proportions.

To one side of the vast hall the wide, arched doors opened into double parlors. On the other side open sliding doors revealed the dining room with its sparkling chandeliers and dish cabinets.

The floors of dark brown stained cypress were almost black from years of polishing. The French windows, with their handsome starched lace curtains, were so spotless that there seemed to be no glass in them. No shutters had been drawn tonight because it was Christmas Eve. In fact, there was no evidence at all that there were any shutters. The deep reveals of the window openings cleverly concealed the shutters which folded back out of sight when they were not in use.

The house, like a human heart, seemed to give of its light and gladness to all the world. Collette danced like a fairy through all the dear, familiar rooms. Pierre felt so deep a peace that all his problems disappeared. Miracles might happen on Christmas Eve.

To Collette he said, "Do you believe in Santa Claus?" as they went in to supper; and when she replied impishly, "Of course," he surprised himself by stating quite soberly, "Well, I do too."

The supper was informal, a delectable spread set out on the dining room table. Both little grandmothers flew here and there, to pour coffee, to serve salad, to urge second helpings of the pink, spiced ham. The Negroes were celebrating in their own cabins after preparing the meal. An air of expectancy hung over everybody and everything, as though good must be heaped on good.

The fragrant balminess of pine and the scent of late garden roses filled the double parlors to which the diners retired with their black sweet coffee in little porcelain cups. Collette drank milk from one of the cups so that she could hold one of the tiny silver saucers in her hand, the saucers with the D'Orsay monogram just the size of the base of the cup.

Firelight danced on the walls over the rich carpets, and upon the polished old furniture.

Tante Bébé was everywhere—until Papa came in from the out-of-doors. Then she followed him about, waiting upon him herself in the dining room and pulling a chair up beside him in the back parlor.

It was wonderful to have everybody together. In a little while the darkies would come to the veranda to sing Christmas carols; but this magic hour was just for the family.

"We'll distribute the gifts under the tree in the morning," Tante Bébé promised. "Tonight I hope you won't mind if I present one gift to one person. It is not really a gift—just the restoration of something that has always belonged to him."

Pierre thought, *This is the miracle.* He watched Tante Bébé take the long, business envelope from the mantel where it had been propped against some holly. He watched her hand it to Papa. Collette nudged Pierre.

"The will?" she whispered.

Pierre shook his head unbelievingly. It couldn't be.

Papa opened the envelope slowly. He merely glanced at the official-looking papers that he drew out.

"A deed to Live Oaks," he said. The children looked their disappointment. "Solidelle, I cannot accept what is not yours to give. But I thank you from the bottom of my heart for your generosity."

"The plantation needs you," Tante Bébé wailed.

"I am willing, even eager, to help you," Papa assured his sister. "After Epiphany and the King Cake sales, I'll come out and spend a few weeks getting things in shape for spring."

"Please make my brother see the light!" Tante Bébé appealed to Mama.

Mama said, "He must do what he thinks is right. I have a notion that we shall find the will at the right time."

"Could it be hidden on the plantation?" Pierre inquired. "After all, the plantation was Grandpère D'Orsay's home."

"Why not forget about the will until after the holidays?" Tante Evangeline suggested. "Now is a time of peace."

But Pierre's thoughts would not be sidetracked. Live Oaks belonged to his father. It belonged to him in the fullest sense of the word. Pierre had made a wonderful discovery: he had seen with his own eyes the way the Negroes depended upon his father and how much Tante Bébé needed to consult him. Why, his father knew all about planting and harvesting and selling. He knew about cotton and sugar-cane and even about the peach and pecan trees. If he did ride a fine horse about the plantation, he did it to be about his business. There was a very real reason now to hunt for the will. Papa so richly deserved the plantation. He hadn't even mentioned the pastry shop since leaving Royal Street.

Pierre went into the great hall and stood looking at the glowing tree. Tante Evangeline and Collette followed him out.

"Did you know, Pierre, that you are to sleep in Grandpère D'Orsay's study tonight?" Tante Evangeline asked. "The desk is very much like the Jaculi desk in the Bayou country. You might even find a secret panel in the wall, and Solidelle says you are to poke around all you please."

Mère came rustling up in her black silk with its delicate white lace at the throat.

"Evangeline has told you?" she inquired. "I thought it would add to your Christmas joy. You see, your Grandpère D'Orsay never lost his love of mystery. You know how a crow does?—tucks things away in queer places. Little boys do, too. Well, Grandpère D'Orsay never did outgrow the crow stage, bless him."

Collette, her eyes on Pierre's glowing face, shouted, "Oh, Pierre, aren't you glad it's Christmas!"

Pierre knew what she meant. Always before he had been allowed to sit in a chair in Grandpère's study or to read a book there. But never had he been allowed to "poke around" as he had wanted to.

His thank-you included Tante Evangeline, Mère, and Christmas itself, as he ran up the stairs to look around the study.

The desk was just as Felix had described it. Quickly he opened one drawer—empty! He tried another. With a quick jerk he pulled out a third. It came out in his hand, and in the back was a little secret compartment. That was for jewels, Pierre remembered. Grandpère's jewel compartment was full of little screws and bolts and nails. Pierre sighed and put the drawer in again. Nothing discovered, yet, but it was fun looking.

He didn't know whether or not Tante Evangeline was teasing about the secret panel, but if Grandpère loved mysteries, as Mère said, surely there was a chance that there might be one. He decided to start examining the wall near the fireplace. It seemed very solid. But suddenly an oblong piece of polished wood along which he was feeling moved—moved so easily that he was startled. Almost he lost his balance on the hassock on which he stood.

Yes, the wood moved, revealing a shallow space in the chimney. Pierre reached in. He brought out several old pipes, prisms of chandeliers, small screw drivers, and various other implements connected with Grandpère's "tinkering." Pierre's fingers encountered last of all some metal disks, not tinny but rich to the touch. Excitedly he drew them out. Why, they were gold pieces! Well, maybe not gold, but they looked like gold—gold coins. And they were pierced, to be sewed on some costume or other, Pierre decided. A Mardi Gras costume! He put the coins back with the pipes and other miscellany.

What a simple, small-boy person Grandpère D'Orsay had been! Pierre felt almost as though the two of them were the same age. It was a strange feeling. He went slowly down the green garlanded stairway when he heard the Negroes coming towards the house, singing in their deep, beautiful voices, "It Came Upon the Midnight Clear."

Mère was at the foot of the stairs.

"Did you make some wonderful discovery, cheri?" Mère asked.

"I found the secret panel and secret drawer," he answered. "But, Mère, did you ever see the desk that Grandpère D'Orsay bought as a gift for Napoleon?"

"I should hope *not!*" Mère's eyes were snapping bright.

"I never was in sympathy with the plot to bring Napoleon to New Orleans."

"Please. I don't want to pry, Mère," Pierre persisted. "But I think it would help to know. You knew about his buying the desk, didn't you, Mère?"

"Certainly I knew about it," Mère admitted. "I heard nothing else for months after it was ordered from the French cabinet maker for fear it should be lost at sea or stolen by rival pirates."

"What do you suppose became of it, Mère?"

"It's probably stored some place. I haven't thought about it in years. Doubtless your grandfather will reveal it in his will—his final will."

"Do you think the final will might be in the desk?"

"It might be, cheri. It seems quite logical that it might be, now that you mention it. What a reasoner you are!"

"I'm not much of a reasoner, Mère; I'm just a guesser."

Mère took Pierre's hand, and together they went out on the wide veranda where the rest of the family were enjoying the singing of the Negroes. Gently now all the voices of the household blended in *"Silent Night, Holy Night. All is calm, all is bright."*

CHAPTER 8

King Cakes

AFTER a day-long drive from the plantation, the D'Orsays were arriving back in New Orleans. As the team clopped wearily over the cobblestones and flagstones, Collette, and Mama too, dozed against Mammy Margot in the back seat. Pierre, beside his father on the front seat, was wide awake with the excitement of being at home again. It was good to hear the deep-throated whistles of the boats and the dimmed shouts of the stevedores from the levee. It was good to smell the familiar odors and to know that a banana boat was in from South America.

Canal Street looked like a glittering, ever-changing fairyland. It was almost as jam-packed with shoppers as though there were a parade. New Orleans had observed Christmas as a religious holiday; New Year's Day, just in the offing, was to be the day for gifts and calling, to be followed by Epiphany with its King Cakes.

The D'Orsays were returning early from Live Oaks, because Papa had to attend to the ordering of materials for the King Cakes. They were expected to be the biggest sales of the year. Everybody bought King Cakes, from the wealthiest families to the poorest Negroes. Papa was planning to set aside stale cakes to be sold for a few pennies to the poorer people.

"Doesn't it seem strange, Papa, to be selling King Cakes instead of buying them?" Pierre mused.

"Seems queer, all right," Papa agreed. "I remember, as a boy, how important our King Cake was. If the Pirate Pastry Shop is going to bake King Cakes, they must be the best."

Papa did not sound especially happy, but he was attacking a job that had to be done with new zest.

"How do you suppose the custom ever started," Pierre inquired, "of eating King Cakes on Epiphany?"

"King Cakes! Cakes for the King, of course, the King in this case being the Christ Child. Epiphany! The day on which the Magi or Wise Men visited the Christ Child, bringing gifts of gold and frankincense and myrrh!" Papa's little black mustache twitched. "In remembrance, we bake King Cakes and place a little gift in each cake. But gold and frankincense and myrrh would hardly be practicable."

"What gift is the Pirate Pastry Shop going to bake in our King Cakes, Papa?" Pierre asked. "The Italian Bakery over on St. Philip baked lucky beans in their cakes last year, and the Dumaine Shop used pecans, right in the shell, you know."

The horses were almost to the Cathedral now, and looking up Pirate's Alley, Pierre could see the shop on Orleans Street, brightly lighted even though it was late.

"I promised Collette," Papa said, as his gaze followed

Pierre's, "that I would use the little toy dolls she so admires. I have a date with her to go to the Miniature Shop after New Year's Day."

The horses began to trot as they turned into St. Ann Street. There was the familiar sound of galeries and sidewalks being sluiced for cleanliness. The shuttered houses showed tiny bars of gold light. Shadowy willows swept down over a crumbling wall.

At last the horses were stabled, the portmanteaux were unpacked, and Collette was tucked into bed. Papa turned to his son who was hesitating on the runway to the garçonnière.

"Too tired to run down to the pastry shop with me?" he inquired.

"Oh, no, Papa. I'd like to go." Pierre felt almost like a partner. Besides, Monsieur Boudro had promised to have a job for him during the holiday vacation.

Late as it was, there was a customer in the shop, a typical tourist in tweeds, with a brown leather bag at his feet. From the crusty odors that filled the shop, it was evident that the French bread was at a critical stage and that André Boudro was nervous over being detained.

"I've never before had trouble finding streets," the tourist was confessing, "but I crossed Royal at Canal and lost it."

The baker's imploring glance came to rest on Pierre who stood beside his father looking into the case.

"Here, sir," he offered, "is the son of the owner. He will tell you all about the streets. Excuse me, *please*."

He motioned to Papa to follow him into the kitchen.

The stranger was quite affable.

"I must have interrupted his kitchen work," he apologized, looking after Monsieur Boudro's departing figure. "Frankly, I'm lost. Once, years ago, I was in New Orleans, to pick up some antiques; but things have changed. Or I have forgotten. Name's Moffet—Dave Moffet. . . . You're young D'Orsay, I take it."

He looked hard at Pierre, as if he were trying to memorize him.

"Yes, sir," Pierre answered. "I think I can set you right, Mr. Moffet. Canal Street, as you know, divides Up Town from Down Town. The French Quarter is Down Town. When our streets cross Canal, they change their names."

"Why?" Mr. Moffet inquired.

"Our Negro mammy says it's for the same reason that people sometimes change their names after they become rich and fashionable, like changing Mary to Marie," Pierre explained.

Mr. Moffet was amused. He took out his notebook and wrote out Pierre's information, setting down the names in their order from the Mississippi.

He repeated after Pierre: "Decatur becomes Magazine, Chartres becomes Camp, Royal becomes St. Charles, Bourbon becomes Carondolet, Dauphine becomes Baronne, and Burgundy becomes University Place. . . . Well, thanks a lot, young man. If ever I can do a favor for you, don't hesitate to call upon me. And have that cook send me a King Cake sometime next week."

He scribbled his name and hotel address on a card.

"Some customers, all they want to do is to visit," Monsieur Boudro grumbled as Pierre appeared in the kitchen. Then he saw the card and the bill in Pierre's hand and murmured, "Oh, well, one must be accommodating."

Papa was smiling over the list of orders for King Cakes. There was a special list from the Tulane district where Dr. Crager and Lotta had been soliciting orders; and Nonc Samuel's friends had not forgotten the brioche.

Pierre stood near the door, waiting for Papa. He was tired from the day's long ride, but he wasn't too sleepy to notice that Papa was really enjoying the prospects of better business over the holidays. This busy season wouldn't last long, though, and if some good fortune didn't turn up soon, all the discouragement would return with renewed strength.

During the next week, Monsieur Boudro kept Pierre so busy, however, that there was no spare time in which to search for a missing desk or a missing will. It was hurry, hurry, hurry all day long. He walked miles to save fares. Every day he rode the Desire or Gentilly car through the Quarter and transferred on Canal Street to the Freret or St. Charles. Once in awhile he was permitted to take a cab.

He came to know the handsome new houses in the Garden District and Audubon Park, set in their lush tropical shrubbery. But always he came home through the small door in the green gate on Royal Street contented with what he had. If the family could only keep just that!

The bakery closed for one day—New Year's Day, a day even more exciting than Christmas. But even then there was so much to do in preparation for the celebration that Pierre had little time to himself. Mammy Margot wasn't able to have as many colored girls as usual to help her, but the results were just as good. Festivities began on New Year's Eve when eggnog and cakes were served after midnight mass, as in France. After breakfast, gifts were distributed to all the family: trinkets, books, scarves knitted by the grandmothers, and always something fine in needlework by Tante Evangeline. Pierre hesitated to carry the exquisitely monogrammed linen handkerchief in his pocket for fear he might lose it. He carried it in his blouse, folded about the sketch of the desk.

Guests flowed in and out of the house all day long.

The D'Orsays made a number of calls themselves, and later the older members of the family all went to the New Year's Ball. Papa looked very handsome in his evening clothes with a gardenia in his buttonhole. And Mama was truly beautiful in her blue velvet evening gown, adorned with her pearls.

A box of pralines arrived for Pierre and Collette. In the box they found a card. It said, "Good fortune is often close at hand. Happy New Year!" It was signed *Josef*.

"He wants us to keep feeling hopeful," Pierre guessed.

"He wants us to keep searching," Collette decided practically.

Epiphany approached close on the heels of the New Year. The baking of the King Cakes had to be begun very early in the week, for it did not seem to be the custom any more to wait for Le Jour des Rois, or the *day* of the Kings, January sixth, to buy them. People were always rushing the seasons, Monsieur Boudro complained.

The King Cakes in the Pirate Pastry Shop were to be large round rings of the finest brioche. While Annette and the Cragers sorted the crystallized fruit and little candies that were to decorate the cakes, and Marie Fortier carefully selected and washed the pecans, Mama, sleeves rolled up, face flushed with excitement, measured the flour, butter, and milk in just the right proportions to make light, fluffy brioche.

Meanwhile Papa took Collette to the Miniature Shop, just around the corner from St. Anthony's Alley on Royal Street, to select the dolls that were to go into the cakes for *the* day.

When they opened the door, a bell tinkled in the living quarters in back. Nobody rushed in to wait on them, though they could hear someone moving about. A very old woman in black silk with a black lace cap on her head, glanced in and called out, "Take your time, *petiot.* Take all the time in the world."

"Merci," Collette called back, then to her father she said, "She's always like that. Usually I can't decide right away, and she knows I'm honest."

Even today, knowing what she wanted, Collette could not resist looking over the bits of furniture, the dogs, the cats, the goats, the alligators, the little men, the birds, and the tiny houses.

But now Madame was beside her and she might as well give her order. Eyes sparkling with excitement, she took a deep breath and said, "I want five hundred dolls, please!"

"Five hundred dolls!" Madame's wrinkles wreathed into smiles: she could play make believe too. "Five hundred dolls would last a little girl a long time."

"But they're not for me," Collette explained. "They're for King Cakes."

"Your mama does not bake five hundred King Cakes!"

"No, my papa does! He has the Pirate Pastry Shop."

Now Madame was delighted. She threw up her hands, and her laughter crackled. Of course. Of course! She brought out boxes and boxes of little china dolls to choose from. Collette chose the kind she had always liked best, a tiny white china doll with black hair and pink cheeks. Papa approved, and after paying Madame and waiting a bit for the package, he and Collette hastened back to the pastry shop.

Monsieur Boudro approved, too. He tied one of his great aprons about Collette and set one of his starchy caps back on her curls while she washed the dolls in the kitchen of the shop.

"Everybody," he declared, "will have a part in the success of the Pirate Pastry Shop. It will prosper—forever."

"Heaven forbid," Papa murmured, raising an expressive black eyebrow as he watched Collette at her task.

As soon as the first cakes were cool, Pierre set out on his deliveries.

And it was mostly King Cakes to be delivered the next few days. He kept a sharp lookout for desks whenever he passed the antique shops or went into any of the old houses. But nowhere did he find a desk that even remotely resembled the one he was looking for. Nor did he find a single clue to the missing will.

Between customers on Epiphany Eve, he sat disconsolately on a high stool behind the counter and studied the sketch. The desk was so distinctive that he felt certain he would

recognize it even if it were terribly old and worn. Or maybe even painted. He was so engrossed, he did not hear the door of the shop open, and was startled when a voice said, "Young D'Orsay, I believe."

Pierre looked up into the face of the tourist who had inquired directions of him the week before. He laid the picture on the counter, striving to remember the man's name.

Now he recalled it as he slid off the stool. "I hope you

had no further trouble finding your way the other day, Mr. Moffet."

"None at all, thank you," replied Mr. Moffet, his eyes glancing quickly from counter to counter. He appeared to be looking for something special, and he even peered into the kitchen through the half-open door. "Do I see some macaroons back there? Fresh ones?"

"They're just out of the oven," Pierre assured him.

"I'd like two dozen, please," he said, and Pierre's heart leaped excitedly as he headed through the door. Macaroons were one of the most expensive items in the shop.

As he came back from the kitchen with the order, Collette literally burst into the shop.

"Mama has an order from a friend in the upper Pontalba and she said I might call for the little cakes and deliver them —two big boxes—hurry, hurry and get them for me, Pierre!" Then her glance fell on Mr. Moffet and she blushed in confusion. "Oh," she said, "I didn't— I'm sorry . . ."

Pierre, laughing, presented Mr. Moffet, who smiled and said, "I have a son not much older than you, and he gets excited, too. As a matter of fact, he is waiting outside for me. We came down to the Quarter to see if we could find an old, old man named Josef Garavalia. I understand that he was once a pirate."

"We know him very well," said Pierre. "He sells pralines in front of the Cathedral and everybody calls him the Praline Man. We have to go by there on our way to deliver these cakes, so if you like, you may come with us and we'll introduce you."

Outside the shop they found Mr. Moffet's son, Billy, and introductions over, Pierre and Collette escorted the Moffets through the alley and around to the front of the Cathedral. The Praline Man sat there on the steps, huddled in a shawl, his basket beside him.

The smile he bestowed on Pierre and Collette froze when he saw who was with them. His sharp old eyes narrowed, opened wide, and narrowed again. His rheumatic knees did not prevent him from springing to his feet.

"Moffet, eh!" he exclaimed. "You don't have to tell me who you are or who the boy is. Moffets!"

"Well, Governor," Billy Moffet remarked with a grimace, "it's plain to me that he doesn't like us."

"Now, now, my man," Mr. Moffet began in a conciliatory tone, "surely you haven't anything against *me*. You've never seen me before."

"You are the son of Pirate Moffet who sailed with Monsieur D'Orsay and me, aren't you?"

"I am."

"Then you are here for no good."

"I am here only to assert my rights," Mr. Moffet said angrily, "and to claim my father's rightful share of the treasures left with D'Orsay. And I want you to help me, old man."

The Praline Man looked at him calmly for a moment before answering. "Your father had no rightful share; he got all that he deserved, and that was nothing."

He resumed his seat on the step, clearly indicating that

he didn't care to speak further with the Moffets now or ever again.

"Well," said Billy cheerfully, confident that his father would win out in the end.

Angry words were on the tip of Pierre's tongue, but Collette was tugging at his sleeve. "Let's go," she begged.

With a final glance at Mr. Moffet, to make sure that he wasn't going to harm Josef, Pierre walked on with Collette.

"I don't like those Moffets," Collette said when they were out of sight of the Cathedral.

"Josef told me once," Pierre began thoughtfully, "that someone else might be after the desk. I wonder if Moffet knows about it."

"Or about the will? Pierre, do you think he'd be after the will, too?" Collette asked anxiously.

"I wish I knew just what he is after," Pierre answered.

They reached the Pontalbas and delivered the cakes. They were walking back when suddenly Pierre grabbed Collette's hand.

"Come on," he shouted, and began walking very fast.

"Why are you hurrying so?" Collette panted.

"I left . . . my picture . . . on the counter," Pierre disclosed, "the picture of the desk."

"Let's run!" Collette shouted.

But when they arrived at the shop, the sketch wasn't there. It wasn't on the counter. It wasn't under the counter. It wasn't *anywhere!*

CHAPTER 9

Discovery

On Epiphany, just before the dinner hour, Pierre stepped wearily into the pastry shop.

"Pierre, you look fagged," Monsieur Boudro said. "You are too weary to do one more little chore?"

"I guess not."

"Marie, on the top floor, has a cold, and I told her I would send her up a King Cake when the last batch was ready. I made her a special small one when I made the big one for your family."

"I'll take it up gladly," Pierre declared. "I shall tease her about it, too, because if she eats her King Cake all alone, she will be sure to find the tiny china doll. Then she can crown herself Epiphany Queen."

Pierre climbed the winding Spanish staircase with its rich mahogany palings set in a wide balustrade—up and up and up. He had almost forgotten how anxious he had been to be in the room where Marie had found the old, wooden pirate.

Reaching the top floor, he tapped on Marie Fortier's door.

She called, "Come in," and he stepped into the beamed attic.

"Happy Epiphany!" he cried, proffering the box containing the King Cake.

"Thank you," she said. "Put it on the table over there, will you, Pierre?"

She had on a smock and was busy at her easel, doing a portrait. But her supper was ready on a candle-lit table in front of the grate, and she was waiting for the coffee to heat. Pierre went forward and laid the box on the edge of the table.

Then—then, after all these weeks and weeks of looking and hoping—at the moment when he least expected it—he SAW THE DESK.

"What's the matter, Pierre?" Marie asked. "You look so—so startled."

Pierre pointed a shaking finger at the desk, set against the side wall beyond the easel. It had a marble top. It was of curly maple. There were diamond inlays all around the front of it.

"Where did you get that desk?" he managed, his throat dry.

"Why, Pierre!" Marie seemed amused. "That desk belongs to your father, I imagine. It has always been here. At least it was here when I moved into the apartment."

For a long moment Pierre stood looking at the desk. It was just as he had visioned it a thousand times, and yet it was more beautiful. The grain of the curly maple of which it was made was one intricate mass of graceful and lovely curves and swirls and knots. But what held Pierre's fascinated gaze was the complicated diamond-shaped inlay formation that outlined it in a broad, handsome band. He went forward and touched the smooth, shining wood.

"May I bring my father and mother and Collette to see it?" he asked Marie.

"Of course you may." Marie was intent on her easel.

"And may I bring the Praline Man?"

"The Praline Man?" Marie stood with her brush poised, and her laughter brimmed over. "By all means bring the Praline Man. And the Hot Tamale Man. And the Chimney Sweep, too, if you wish."

"I am not joking," Pierre said. "I cannot explain everything to you now, but I have a very good reason for wanting to bring the Praline Man."

"I'm sure you have." Marie humored Pierre. There was a secret little smile about her mouth. "My cold is so much better that I am going to deliver this portrait tonight. I am just retouching it a little. Perhaps you would like to bring everybody up here while I am gone. I shall leave the key under the mat outside my door."

"Oh, thank you," Pierre cried.

He took the steps, running down the first flight, then sliding down the banisters for the last two stories. Ah! What wonderful curves! What a wonderful flight of stairs, leading straight up to Heaven and straight down to Heaven too! What wonderful news to carry home!

He put his head in at the pastry shop kitchen, shouting, "Good-night, Monsieur Boudro! Good-night! And Happy Epiphany!"

Monsieur Boudro lifted his hands in astonishment.

"What happens?" he exclaimed. "A miracle?"

"A miracle!" Pierre cried.

At a walking run he hurried along Orleans Street and saluted Pirate's Alley as he rounded the corner on Royal Street. Good old Pirate's Alley through which so many customers had come to buy King Cakes!

And a King Cake had helped him find the desk. *The* desk. He was no longer the boy whose tired feet had limped into the Pirate Pastry Shop a few minutes before. There were wings on his feet now.

Collette heard her brother's flying steps on the runway and rushed across the patio to greet him as he burst in.

"You found it!" she screeched.

"Yes, I found it!" Pierre shouted. "I found the desk!"

"Where did you find it?" Collette yelled at the top of her voice, and without waiting for a reply, she danced about, screeching, "Pierre found the desk, found the desk, found the desk!"

Mammy Margot bustled out from the kitchen, a ladle in her hand. Toby, a big apron tied about his waist and brandishing a knife, followed behind her, grinning. On the galerie of the garçonnière Nonc Samuel appeared, buttoning his coat and shouting, "What *is* this?"

Out from the house came Mama, stepping lightly and swiftly down the stairs to the patio, and behind her came Papa who had just finished shaving.

"What has happened, cheri?" Mama demanded; and Papa echoed her question.

"Pierre has found the desk," Collette explained, her voice hoarse from shouting.

Pierre, finding himself the center of the family group, was suddenly embarrassed. Even the two grandmothers had appeared in the door of the house and were calling out, "What has happened?"

Nonc Samuel clattered down the steps of the runway and took matters into his own hands. He lifted Pierre onto the wrought iron table in the middle of the patio and said distinctly, "Whatever it is, Pierre, tell the world!"

"I have found the desk," Pierre said, looking down at Papa and speaking directly to him.

"What desk?" Papa asked. Of course he couldn't believe that they had found *the* desk.

"The desk Grandpère D'Orsay bought as a gift for Napoleon," Pierre explained, breathlessly. "It has the same marble top, the same curly maple wood, the same inlays as the picture of it."

Papa was pretending to be calm, but his mustache twitched. He asked quietly, "Where did you find it?"

Pierre took a long breath; they were all watching him and waiting.

"In the attic of the Orleans Street house that you, Papa, received as a christening gift—where Marie has her studio," Pierre explained. "Monsieur Boudro asked me to take a King Cake up to her studio—and there it was. *There it was!* Marie said it had always been there."

"It's the right desk, I think, cheri," Mère decided. "That house was the only city property Grandpère D'Orsay owned besides this Royal Street house. We often sent furniture from the plantation to help furnish the apartments. It would have been easy enough to slip a desk in there, a desk that was bound to cause trouble."

"Now let's not get excited." Papa interrupted the chattering that followed Mère's remarks. "Let's be very businesslike about this. . . . I believe we are having an early dinner tonight so that Tante Bébé and Tante Evangeline may go to an Epiphany party. Also I understand that Collette is going to dance in an operetta, to the delight of her grandmothers. So Mama and Pierre and I will go down to the pastry shop and investigate the desk."

"I'd rather see the desk than dance in the operetta," Collette wailed.

"I'd rather go, too," Tante Bébé decided. "I don't care for Epiphany parties."

"Nor I," Tante Evangeline agreed.

"The entire family," Papa declared severely, "cannot pound up those two flights of stairs, causing commotion. It is just as well not to let even the people in the house know about this—until *we* know."

No dinner since the night Monsieur La Branche had revealed the state of the family finances was so exciting as this meal. Mammy Margot, hovering proudly over Pierre, forgot the sauces until Mama reminded her.

But she did not forget the big, round King Cake with its sprinkling of candied fruits, placed before Mama to cut.

"Be careful, everybody!" Mama warned. "Don't bite the little china doll that has been baked in the cake. It will be in one of the pieces. Whoever finds it will be crowned King or Queen."

Toby had brought in the gold paper crown that could be adjusted to fit anybody's head. He laid it down at Mama's place.

Everybody ate slowly, pulling the cake-like dough apart. Papa, who was more thoughtful than the rest, said, "Immediately after you finish your King Cake, Pierre, I wish you'd run over to the Praline Man's and ask him to meet us at the pastry shop. The picture he gave you will be additional help in identifying the desk. And he will remember."

"But, Papa, I haven't found the picture yet," Pierre said miserably.

"Finding the will in the desk should prove the most satisfactory identification," Nonc decided. "Eh, Pierre?"

"That would be wonderful," Pierre acknowledged.

"If it's the right time," Grand'mère said gently, and Mère nodded accord.

Collette gave a wildly exultant cry.

"I found the doll!" She held up the little china doll she had found in her piece of King Cake and began to lick off the crumbs that clung to it. "Now I can be Epiphany Queen —though I really think Pierre should be, after finding the desk."

"No, thanks," Pierre said. "I wouldn't make a good Queen."

He got up, picked up the paper crown and setting it back on his sister's curls, sing-songed, "Collette D'Orsay, beauteous maiden, I now proclaim you Epiphany Queen! Long may you reign!"

Then Mammy Margot led the Queen away to get dressed for the operetta, and Pierre went out on his errand.

He walked along Dumaine Street in the dusk, past the oldest house in the Mississippi Valley, a house made of soft brick and plaster, the timbers put together with wooden pegs. There had been pegs in the rafters of the house on Orleans Street. Perhaps the house was almost as old as this house of Jean Pascal's. At least it was older than the plot to rescue Napoleon and bring him to New Orleans.

Crossing over to St. Philip, Pierre had no difficulty in locating the faded green gate in the gray plaster wall. Again he climbed the rickety stairs as he had done before, but with a little more confidence. Besides there was a real purpose in his seeing the Praline Man tonight.

The rich, sweet odor of candy cooking met him on the runway of the third story.

When he knocked on the kitchen door, the Praline Man shouted, "Come in!" and as Pierre came through into the front room, added, "Just in time to help."

Josef was dipping small ladles of nut-filled, sugar-brown candy onto the marble slab. The candy was spreading to flat, pancake-like cakes and congealing as it cooled into shiny, bumpy disks.

"Want to help wrap?" He indicated a pile of wax paper, cut into squares.

While Pierre worked, he told the Praline Man about the discovery of the desk, and then he gave him Papa's message.

"Of course!" Josef's smile was eager, and Pierre realized that he was greatly pleased. "Of course. We go at once."

"Just a moment." Pierre hesitated. "I must tell you. I lost the picture of the desk. On the day that Mr. Moffet came to ask about you, I laid it on the counter and . . ."

Josef let out a roar.

"Enough!" he cried. "I know where it is!"

But he would not discuss the matter further with Pierre.

Papa and Mama were already waiting in the Pirate Pastry Shop when Pierre arrived with the Praline Man.

"Set your basket on the counter," Papa invited. "Monsieur Boudro will sell pralines for you while you are busy with us upstairs."

Josef did as Papa requested, but he seemed to have something on his mind.

"May I confess something first, Monsieur D'Orsay?" he inquired, hesitantly. "It is something that may prove to be important. This is it: in moving the desk I nicked one of the little pieces of wood that helps to form one of the diamond-shaped inlays. . . . May I show you? It is at the right corner."

He drew a diagram on some wrapping paper Papa offered him.

Pierre thought they would never get through discussing that flaw. He led the way with Mama up the long flights of stairs. Slowly. Slowly. Mama paused often, to look down the deep well, to admire the balustrade, to remark about the fine, wide treads of cypress.

The key was under the mat as Marie had promised it would be. Pierre turned the lock and went in. He was trembling. What if the desk wasn't really there?

But it was there against the wall, with the flicker of firelight shining on it. There was no electricity on the top floor, but Papa lit the large oil lamp and the candles on the mantel.

"So this is it," Mama said softly, touching the desk; and Papa, his arm around her shoulders, echoed her words, "So this is it."

"It's the desk all right!" Josef shouted. "Look, Monsieur! Look, Madame! Here is the little piece of inlay that I nicked. Come closer, Pierre!"

It was *the* desk, no question about it.

Papa took a long breath. He let down the writing surface while Pierre tried to warm his hands together, waiting.

Then Papa opened the two drawers, swiftly, nervously.

He said, "The drawers fit perfectly, and they slide way to the back of the desk. They leave no space for a false or secret compartment of any kind."

He did not have to add, "But there is nothing in them," for his voice told that.

Then he opened the door below, and the only sound in the room was the crackle of the fire when the Praline Man laid on fresh fuel.

The space for books and papers was empty, too!

Mama, almost in tears, put her arm about Pierre.

"To think, cheri," she comforted, "that you should have found the desk, the famous desk! It does not matter that it does not contain the will."

Pierre could not speak. He blew out the candles while his father turned down the lamp. He was glad of the few moments' gloom. . . . He it was who locked the door and placed the key under the mat again. Then they all went silently down the stairs.

Back in the shop the Praline Man tried to be jovial.

"Have a praline, Pierre," he invited, picking up his basket.

"No, thanks, sir," was all Pierre could manage.

"Don't worry, cheri," Papa soothed. "The desk will bring a fine price if we need more money. There was a fellow in here late this afternoon inquiring about just such a desk—name of Moffet."

Pierre thought the Praline Man was going to have an apoplectic fit. His face grew fiery red under the tan.

"No!" he shouted. "By all that's good and holy! Never sell that desk to a Moffet!"

CHAPTER 10

Poor Boy Sandwiches

THE holiday season was over all too soon, and Pierre and Collette returned to their school-day routine. Mardi Gras was the next event on the festive calendar, but each day something new and exciting was happening at home or at the shop so that the children had no time to spend planning their costumes. Usually they had that problem settled well in advance of the day itself.

Pierre's thoughts were far from costumes and celebrations as he walked home from school one afternoon. His disappointment over his failure to find the missing will was so deep that he could not talk of it, even to Collette. To have found the desk after weeks of searching, and not to have found the will! Spring would be here soon and Papa would be badly needed on the plantation. Monsieur Boudro was a good baker, but he frankly admitted that he was no business man. Lotta Crager was a good bookkeeper, but a bookkeeper is not a buyer. The pastry shop could not go on if Papa wasn't there to manage.

Meanwhile, very little money was coming in. Pierre and

Collette were on the alert for talk concerning the sale of the Royal Street house. They heard not a word. It was as though Mama had decided not to speak of it at all "in front of the children." Both Pierre and Collette knew, however, that it was a very real possibility. They also knew, that no matter what happened, it was only in the Quarter that they could feel at home.

Pierre passed Jackson Park. He hadn't been there since the day he had played "Hide the ball." Today was the anniversary of the Battle of New Orleans, and the Square was filled with people. He stopped to watch. A band was playing; there was a small parade, and Marie Fortier, from a platform, was placing a wreath around the neck of the rearing steed of Stonewall Jackson.

Pierre saw Gaston Sevier coming towards him. He didn't feel like talking to Gaston, but he greeted him politely.

"They didn't have a platform the day you climbed up, did they, Pierre?" Gaston teased.

"No," Pierre admitted. "That was a long time ago."

"Long time ago!" Gaston mimicked. "A little over two months."

"Oh, go away," Pierre mumbled.

"What's the matter with you?" Gaston's curiosity was aroused. Pierre walked away without answering, but like a bur, Gaston stuck to him and followed him all the way to the pastry shop.

Monsieur Boudro was behind the counter when the boys came in. Gaston looked into the cases, exclaiming, "Poor Boy Sandwich loaves!"

"You want a loaf?" Monsieur Boudro inquired, reaching for a yard-long loaf.

"No, thanks," Gaston said with a grin. "I don't indulge." He had just come in to snoop around, not to buy anything.

"Where's Papa, Monsieur Boudro?" Pierre inquired.

"Important visitors!" The baker poked his finger towards the ceiling. "Upstairs!"

"Who are they?" Pierre asked. Gaston was at his side.

"Two experts. One is from Feldman, one from Rothschild. . . ."

"What have you got upstairs that's so valuable it has to be appraised by experts?" Gaston inquired quickly.

"We got . . ." Monsieur Boudro began.

"Don't tell him," Pierre begged.

In a few moments Papa came into the shop, accompanied by two smiling men.

"We're going out for coffee," Papa informed Monsieur Boudro. He patted Pierre's shoulder. "Good work, son. You found the authentic desk all right."

"What is this? What is this?" Gaston demanded.

May as well tell him and get rid of him, Pierre thought. "Oh," he said nonchalantly, "just a desk that my Grandfather D'Orsay bought for Napoleon. It was to be a gift for the Emperor when he arrived in New Orleans."

"Say," Gaston's eyes opened wide, "I want to see that. That must be the desk Billy Moffet was telling me about."

"What!" Pierre shouted in amazement. "How do you know Billy?"

Now Gaston was nonchalant. "My father is a very important banker, you know; he has business with lots of people."

Pierre could have bitten his tongue for telling Gaston where the desk was. Now Gaston would tell the Moffets and Mr. Moffet would be around to lay his hands on it.

"Let me see it," Gaston begged.

"No!" Pierre's shout was so loud and angry that Gaston gave him one puzzled glance and left the shop without another word.

Pierre waited around for his father. He wanted to ask him not to let anyone see the desk until Grandpère's will was found. He didn't know just why he felt that way, but he was sure that once Grandpère D'Orsay's desk was gone, the will would never be found.

But Papa didn't seem to be coming back, and Pierre grew tired waiting. He was anxious to get home anyway and to tell Collette about Gaston. He always told Collette everything, for he had learned that sometimes she had some very good ideas.

He found Collette in the patio, and together they went into the house to discuss their problems. Pierre told her that the desk wasn't safe as long as the Moffets knew where it was.

"We must tell Marie, then, not to let anybody in unless Papa is there," Collette decided.

"Suppose Papa wants to sell the desk to Mr. Moffet?" Pierre asked. "Moffet is a collector of antiques, you know."

"Well, we couldn't help that, I guess; but I heard Mama tell him that if he could manage until after Mardi Gras, he shouldn't do anything to make us unhappy."

"Make *us* unhappy?" Pierre questioned in surprise.

"Mama knows how we feel about the desk, I guess," Collette answered.

"Then we can keep the Moffets from the desk until that time, at least," Pierre shouted happily. "And maybe by then we'll find the will."

Collette nodded in agreement. "Pierre, do you remember the secret panel you found in Grandpère's study at the plantation?"

"Uh-huh." Pierre wondered what she was getting at.

"Well," Collette continued slowly, "maybe there's a secret panel in Marie Fortier's studio. Remember the wooden pirate? And the desk is there—and maybe there's a hidden panel there too."

"Yippee!" Pierre almost squeezed the breath out of Collette with his big hug. "That is an idea, Collette. A wonderful idea. I had always meant to give that place a good search but never got around to it. We'll look tomorrow."

"Tomorrow's Sunday. We can't disturb Marie on Sunday," Collette reminded.

"Well, Monday, then. If it's there, it will still be there on Monday."

"Chi-ll-ll-un." That was Mammy Margot's voice interrupting them to get ready for supper. Pierre ran to his room, whistling gaily.

After supper, Nonc asked Pierre and Collette if they would like to walk over to Canal Street to see the bright lights. They were both eager, but Mama said that Collette looked too tired and would have to go to bed early. But Pierre could go if he liked.

It was exciting to parade on the wide, sparkling boulevard, to be part of the great crowd that window-shopped or stopped in restaurants for food and drink. But it was not until much later, when the two of them had gone back into the Quarter and were seated at a counter in a little, all-night restaurant on Dumaine Street, that Nonc hinted what was on his mind.

"Pierre," he said, "this was the place your grandfather visited on Saturday nights—whenever he was in town. He liked people; he talked with everybody."

Pierre himself could understand his grandfather's interest in the crowd. He watched the tired farmers, the stevedores weary from unloading bananas and shrimp and coffee, and the soldiers and sailors enjoying port food. He liked the chatter around him, Greek, Spanish, Cajun French, and Italian. These men were all honestly hungry. The place was steamy with jambalaya, hot and savory of garlic, tomatoes, and onions. Nonc took a cup of the strong, black coffee.

From behind the counter the stout old Frenchman, Anton, inquired, "Qu'est-ce que c'est? What is it?"

Pierre liked the immense apron and the large, starched cap, askew. Probably the cap had been askew when Grand-père D'Orsay patronized the place.

"Poor Boy Sandwiches," Nonc ordered.

"The beeg bread? The leetle bread?"

"What do *you* think—with a boy like this?"

"Beeg!" Anton laughed his ruddy laugh.

He picked up a yard-long loaf, cut it across, then slit it the long way. He buttered both sides lightly. On the lower half he laid slices of cold meat, slices of tomato, some cold vegetables, bits of pickle and olive, and a little green salad. Finally he set the top on. Here was a whole meal. Nonc accepted his solemnly.

Pierre bit into his; it was good, uncommonly good. For a dime no man could ask for better.

When Anton finally achieved a spot of leisure, Nonc asked, "Anton, who invented the Poor Boy Sandwich?"

Anton's mirthful laugh had some bluster in it.

"How I guess!" he shouted. "Somebody beeg! Somebody nize! Somebody that hate to see peoples hongry!"

Then he turned back to his fat kettle in which he had fried fish and began to ladle in a cornmeal mixture—hush puppies. He lifted the light, doughnut-like cakes onto the platter of fish. Having served the impatient stevedores, he relaxed his old body on a stool with a sigh of weariness. He was not so young any more.

"Anton," Nonc asked, conversationally, "do you remember Monsieur D'Orsay of Live Oaks?"

"Do . . . I . . . remember?" Anton's wrinkled old face lit up with the sunshine of his memories. "I remember—like yesterday."

He remembered every cotton crop and every failure of tobacco or sugar cane. He remembered the good years and the bad years. He knew the Negro servants. Nonc led the garrulous old man on, hoping for something revealing.

Then Pierre wedged in a question.

"Do you remember," he asked, "my grandfather's ever telling you about how he hid things?"

"Hid things?" Anton looked ceilingward, shook his head, and then chuckled as he said, "Not much. Only same tall tale all a time! He say he have a magic spring—he touch—voila! Suddenly a little box appear. He know I do not believe; he laugh, too."

"That was a tall tale, wasn't it!" Nonc remarked as he and Pierre walked home under the stars, bright between the narrow streets with their overhanging galeries, the lace making patterned shadows on the streets.

"I believe it," Pierre said with decision. "I'm going to look around for magic springs."

Tourists

Pierre's earnest hope that the whereabouts of the desk would be kept fairly secret until after Mardi Gras was completely shattered when he saw the Sunday paper. Reporters had done their work well, for there, in large black letters, stood the caption:

PIRATE PASTRY SHOP HOUSES GIFT FOR NAPOLEON

The article revealed the fact that the desk had been discovered in the studio of Marie Fortier on the top floor of the Orleans house. Collectors, it was stated, were bidding for the fabulous piece.

"I bet those collectors are Papa's experts," Pierre grumbled, picking up the paper again from the breakfast table.

Collette was standing behind Pierre's chair, reading over his shoulder. "Oh, Pierre, now everybody knows," she wailed.

"Everybody knows what, cherie?" Papa looked up from his book.

"About the desk," Pierre and Collette answered together.

"Well, you didn't expect something related to Napoleon to be kept secret, did you?" Papa laughed.

"We did feel," Pierre began timidly, "that we should keep it as much of a secret as possible until we find the will."

"We went through the desk. The will's not there. You know that, Pierre."

"I know, Papa, but this is something I feel. It's a hunch. . . ."

"I just know the desk will help us find the will," Collette helped out.

"We can't live on feelings and hunches, children," Papa said sadly and went back to his book.

"You won't ever sell the desk to the Moffets, though, will you?" Pierre asked anxiously, remembering the Praline Man's fervent words. *Never sell that desk to a Moffet.*

"Play along with your hunches until after Mardi Gras, and maybe until spring. Then we'll see," Papa answered, without looking up.

"That's that, I guess," Pierre said under his breath.

"Maybe we'll find a secret panel in Marie's studio tomorrow," Collette reminded her brother in a whisper.

Monday morning Collette and Pierre made arrangements to meet at the pastry shop after school. Neither of them had counted on so many other people being at the shop, too. The publicity in the Sunday papers had quick results, and when Pierre arrived at the Pirate Pastry Shop, he saw not

Collette but a whole group of tourists led by a Bally-hoo Man. The guide was pointing at the windows of Marie Fortier's study.

"Up there, ladies and gentlemen," he rumbled, "you will find the famous desk that Monsieur D'Orsay bought as a gift for the great Napoleon. The old gentleman D'Orsay, it is said, was a gallant pirate; and this shop, named in honor of the business he carried on, is still run by his descendants. . . ."

Pierre dashed into the shop, trembling with anger. He hated to have family affairs broadcast publicly. Collette, who had come in earlier, came running from the kitchen to meet him.

"Pierre, do you think all those people will go up to see the desk? Oh, stop them, Pierre, you must stop them."

"It's our desk and not for sale. I will stop them," Pierre said with determination.

Just then the shop door opened and in came the guide followed by all the strangers, laughing and talking. Monsieur Boudro met the crowd and called to Papa in the back room. A number of tourists bought pastry while the guide asked Papa if he would take them up to look at the desk.

Papa was silent for a minute. He watched the sales of cakes thoughtfully, and decided that this was just what he wanted—to encourage tourists to pass his way.

"I'm afraid that the entire crowd is a little too large for you to take up. But if Miss Fortier is in, I see no reason why you can't take two or three of those most interested. One moment, if you please. Oh, Pierre, will you run upstairs and ask Marie if she will allow a few people in to see the desk right now?"

Pierre stood unhappily by the door, not moving.

"Did you hear, Pierre? Quickly now."

Pierre went to the hall stairs with Collette at his heels.

"What will you do?" Collette asked.

"I don't know. I don't want to disobey Papa, but he doesn't understand how important it is that no one see the desk until we find the will. If we let any old person come snooping around, asking the price, poking all over, we'll never get a chance to find the will before spring."

"But what will you tell Papa and that guide?" Collette worried.

They were both still standing at the head of the stairs when the guide and three tourists came up to them. The guide looked at Pierre's troubled frown and immediately came to his own conclusion.

"We can't go up now, eh?" he said, turning to the tourists with a shrug.

Collette opened her mouth to speak but Pierre gave her a sharp glance just in time.

"I'm very sorry, sir, but I . . ." Pierre began to explain.

"That's all right, young fellow," one of the tourists said, "we can't go around bothering private citizens. We understand."

And they walked out.

When they were out of sight the children relaxed.

"That was easier than I expected," Pierre grinned.

"Wasn't it funny?" Collette began, laughing. "He told us

before we had a chance to tell him. Let's go up ourselves and see if we can look for that panel now."

Marie was surprised and amused when they asked if they might examine the walls; but when they explained the situation to her, she was pleased to let them. She even promised not to allow visitors in to see the desk.

"But," she warned them, "your father said that he was going to bring several people in to look at the desk and he believes that some of them will want me to paint their portraits. I'll have to let them in, won't I?"

They agreed to that. Hastily they set to work examining the walls. They tapped and pushed and felt around all the edges, but nothing moved. They worked especially hard on the wall by the desk, but no luck.

"Guess we'd better go down, now," Collette said after a while. "Papa will be wondering what became of us." They thanked Marie and said good-by. It had been a good idea. Unfortunately it had yielded nothing.

The one result of Pierre's encounter with the tourists was that the Bally-hoo Man systematically avoided the Pirate Pastry Shop. No groups of strangers came to see and possibly to bid for the desk, true; but neither did they buy pastry. Each day Papa complained a little more loudly than usual that the Pirate Pastry Shop was a headache. Monsieur Boudro said it was a heartache. For Pierre and Collette it was both.

"It looks," Collette decided one afternoon, several days

later, "as if Papa will have to run the pastry shop indefinitely. Nice big word, that—indefinitely."

"Maybe something will happen today," Pierre said without much hope. "I'm going down to the shop now. Monsieur Boudro might need some help."

Collette wished him luck.

Monsieur Boudro did have an errand for Pierre. He was waiting for him to take some cakes up to Marie. Pierre gladly climbed the stairs with a sample of chestnut cakes, covered with delectable, squashy pink frosting. He was amazed to find Marie busy on a painting of—of all things—the desk.

"I'm doing it out of gratitude to you and the desk," she explained. "It has brought me such good luck. Your father has brought a number of people to see the desk, as he promised, and several of them asked to have their portraits done. If it hadn't been for the desk and your finding it right here in this room, I might have gone on living on Poor Boy Sandwiches. Now I eat cake!"

"And to think," Pierre lamented, "that I was so careless as to lose the sketch. The clue to the missing will must have been on it somewhere. This was where Grandpère used to come to be alone, and there's no other place where he could have kept it."

"Don't worry so about it, Pierre," Marie comforted. "See what a picture I am making of it instead. Maybe we will find the secret yet."

Pierre went to Marie's side and looked at the canvas. "I

never thought that a piece of furniture could be a portrait," he marveled.

"The desk has personality." Marie appraised her work. "I set it in that golden light to accent the light wood, and I made the shadows purple—the color of royalty. But it's not finished."

"I see," Pierre said, "you've got all that detail left to put in with those diamond-shaped mosaics. Imagine a cabinet maker putting that much work on a decoration." He started towards the door, then turned back. "What are you going to do with your picture, Marie?"

"Offer it at the Spring Fiesta sale," Marie answered. "I want it hung in Pirate's Alley along with the paintings of all the other artists in the Quarter. And I want it offered at auction, even if it brings only fifty cents. 'Portrait of a Desk'—fifty cents!"

"I'll save up my nickels and bid for it myself," Pierre decided.

Marie thanked him for that with a warm smile, and he left, feeling more hopeful. Even Marie was doing her best to help them find the will.

When he returned home late that afternoon, he found that Tante Bébé had returned from Live Oaks, bringing with her a huge box of materials out of which they were to fashion Mardi Gras costumes. All troubles were forgotten in the excitement. Besides, Papa had promised there'd be no sale until after Mardi Gras.

CHAPTER 12

Mardi Gras

It was the hat that decided Pierre D'Orsay's costume for Mardi Gras. The moment he caught sight of it in the box that Tante Bébé had brought from Live Oaks, he pounced upon it. It was of soft red velvet, like the sixteenth century velvet in Rothschild's, and it was decorated with gold coins around the rim and on the silken cords that tied it, coins exactly like those Pierre had found behind the secret panel on the plantation.

Tante Evangeline agreed to fashion some breeches and a blouse to match, and Mama said she'd find a gold scarf to belt the costume.

"Dig down," Tante Bébé suggested, "and you'll probably find some boots. This old stuff was in Grandpère D'Orsay's armoire. I believe he kept every outfit from the first parade to the last. During these hard times, it's just as well to use what we have instead of renting costumes."

"I'll have to rent a mask," Pierre decided. "I'm afraid I don't look much like a bold, bad pirate. I haven't any mustaches."

"There are lots of other characteristics that you lack too," Tante Bébé teased. "You lack a scowl and a swagger."

Mère came out in the patio to look at the souvenirs of Grandpère D'Orsay's Fat Tuesdays. She approved Pierre's choice.

"Your grandfather prized that hat highly," she recalled. "He brought it home after an encounter at sea with pirates. Seems to me that he owned other things with that same decoration. Take good care of the hat, Pierre."

"Indeed I will, Mère," Pierre promised.

For several weeks the grown-ups had been going off to the Carnival Season balls, Tante Bébé and Tante Evangeline looking like princesses in their finest gowns. Their escorts were always handsome Creoles of neighborhood families, and the house was always redolent of perfume and flowers and filled with laughter. There had been evening parades too, and little parties. But now the great day, the day of days, had arrived, Fat Tuesday. On the calendars it was only Tuesday, February 19, 1901, but to New Orleaneans, it was the greatest day for fun in all the year.

Since Sunday evening the city had been set to the tune of gayety, and band music reached the house on Royal Street almost continuously. The only worry was the weather.

A pleasant wind filled the patio while overhead ragged white clouds threatened rain. Mammy Margot shook her head dolefully as she saw the D'Orsays off for the day.

"De las' time you-all folkses kin cut high jinks befo' Lent begins!" she fussed. "Eff'n hit rains, the parade'll be spoilt."

"If it rains," Papa said, "the Pirate Pastry Shop will be

packed to the doors—but not with customers. Besides there are going to be two big parades, Rex in the daytime and Comus at night. The 1901 theme for Rex is 'Human Passions and Characteristics,' and for Comus it is 'Selections from the Opera.' But we won't be educated either in a way of life or in music, so we shall go ahead and have a good time. And you have a good time too, Mammy Margot."

Mammy Margot had this day off herself, for the Negroes celebrated their own Mardi Gras. She was in no hurry, however, as she softly patted Collette's blue ribbon bow into place, setting a flower-trimmed hat carefully over it. Collette was not to get into her fairy costume until evening when she would ride on a Comus float. Then Mammy Margot tilted Pierre's brim at a more rakish angle as she said, "Ah 'clare, Massah Pierre, eff'n yo' ain't a bo'n pirate!" The grandmothers waved good-by. They were not equal to more than one parade and would rest until evening. Their real celebration had taken place the night before when they went to the French Opera, sitting side by side on the fourth level of seats.

Everywhere, in parks and on boulevards, the azaleas had been in bloom since Saint Valentine's Day. They were now past their prime; but to visitors from snow-bound Minnesota and Wisconsin, they looked like marvels of beauty. The bright flowers, the walls green with vines or colorful with flowers, the patios into which visitors were allowed to peek, filled with beauty—what a day to be glad in! And what a place to be glad in!

Collette and the aunts took a cab with Mama, but Pierre

hurried along Royal Street on foot. He loitered only long enough to greet the old man in the Coin Shop. Usually the old man's gray head was bent over his collection of rare

coins, but today he stood in the doorway of his shop; today he was a citizen of the City that Care Forgot. Today he must celebrate.

"Aren't you going to mask, Monsieur?" Pierre called out. "Aren't you going down to the waterfront to see Rex arrive by boat?"

The old man shook his head, glanced at Pierre, then continued to stare.

"What is that costume you are wearing?" he inquired.

"I'm a pirate," Pierre explained, "except for my face. But I'm on my way to the Costumer's now, to buy a mask."

"That hat! Surely you didn't get *that* at a Costumer's."

"Oh, no," Pierre informed him. "This hat belonged to my Grandpère D'Orsay."

"It has an ancient and honorable appearance. Take good care of it."

"Yes, sir."

Pierre crossed over to Bourbon Street to buy his mask.

Strung across the Costumer's Shop were strange masks of every kind, clowns, cowboys, fat boys, devils, animals, Indians, Chinese, and, yes, pirates! Like all the other shops this little place was decorated with yellow, green, and purple bunting, the carnival colors.

To try on the mask, the dealer lifted off Pierre's hat, but Pierre took it from him and held it clasped to his chest. The dealer grinned.

"Told to watch your hat, eh?" he chuckled. "Well, you don't have to worry about it here."

From the corner of Orleans Street at Bourbon, Pierre could see people swarming in and out of the pastry shop. Too busy to try to get into the crowded restaurants, many tourists ate brioche and cake on the streets. Good Mardi Gras patronage paid for many a slack month in business.

Everybody was in costume, and it looked funny to see masks tilted back, heads of crocodiles and bears and red-nosed policemen, while mouths underneath consumed quantities of pastry.

Pierre crowded into the Pirate Pastry Shop between a street vendor with a bouquet of balloons and an organ grinder with a monkey. The monkey reached out an inquisitive paw for Pierre's hat, and Pierre took off his tempting headpiece and tucked it under his arm.

Papa, in pirate costume—everyone associated with the Pirate Pastry Shop was in pirate costume—came into the shop from the little back room with Mr. Moffet and his son, Billy, both dressed in velvet and lace like noblemen of old. Pierre's heart sank. Then he noticed the dour looks of both Moffets, and he realized that Papa had not set a price on the desk.

The Moffets left the shop without looking at Pierre.

"Coming with me, Papa?" Pierre asked.

"I'm taking Mama and Collette," Papa said. "Run along, cheri. You'll meet lots of your friends. Anyway, in a Mardi Gras crowd, he travels fastest who travels alone. Listen to those whistles!"

Never had a king from a fabulous, distant clime arrived in any city with greater pomp and circumstance. Cannon were already booming in Jackson Park as Pierre crossed through. On the river, craft of all types had formed a double line, tooting and whistling with all their might. Tugboats, steamboats, battleships, and yachts were packed with spectators waving at the shore crowds; and the closely packed banks of people waved back as one person. There was a great flutter of banners and flags and pennants on the ships;

there was a great flutter of handkerchiefs from the cheering crowds.

Pierre ducked here and there, trying to see the royal yacht as it reached the double line of vessels. But all he could see was the gray smoke from the various boats, and the clouds above him.

Suddenly rain broke out, and a high wind swept the levee. The crowd rolled back like a great wave. Pierre tucked his hat under his blouse and made his way forward to where the crowd had thinned. The King, in state on his yacht, had received proper homage and was now reaching the docks. The fifteen minute shower was over. People surged back to the docks, but Pierre had won a place of vantage. Fanfare, music, artillery and infantry waiting, and the King mounting his throne!

The sun came out as if to highlight the canopy of glittering blue and gold-rose behind the monarch who was in a costume of the Middle Ages. It was of velvet richly trimmed with ermine, gems, and gold lace; and light danced from the gleaming dagger and shining scepter. Two maskers at the King's feet supported banners bearing the royal arms, and two lions, that looked almost real, held garlands. Everything was silver and gold and sparkling colors.

On his float the King led the procession past City Hall where Mayor Capdeville handed him the keys to the city through an intermediary. Pierre could not get close enough to see this ceremony, but it did not matter. He could see the floats of the Rex parade above the heads of the crowd.

Afterwards it took him fully an hour to wedge his way

through the crowds on Canal Street. Here there were any number of impromptu parades going on. A band would strike up, somebody would start a drill, and the crowd would cheer. Pierre was fascinated by a fife and drum corps augmented by bagpipes. Men and women in kilts were doing a highland fling. . . . Someone reached over and touched Pierre's shoulder. It was Billy Moffet.

"Want to do a little business with you," he announced.

"Do you?" Pierre's eyes were on the dance.

"I've decided to buy your hat," Billy said, pushing in beside Pierre.

He said it arrogantly and with certainty; and Pierre felt irritated all out of proportion.

"Sorry, but it's not for sale," he said stiffly.

"Don't be silly." It was Billy's turn to be irritated. "It's nothing but an old hat that you'll wear only to parades. I can pay you plenty for it."

"What do you mean by plenty?"

Billy held a roll of bills down at his side, for Pierre to see. Lace fell over the hand from the blue velvet coat.

"I wouldn't cheat you," Pierre said and, when Billy began to argue, slid through the crowd.

He had reached the orange juice and pineapple stand across the street and was having a drink when he saw the Praline Man a few feet away. He wore a pirate mask, but no special costume, just the baggy velvet trousers and coat and a red scarf. Pierre was about to address him when some school friends came along. He joined them, weaving in and out of the crowds.

Pierre hoped Anton was in the crowd. The magic spring that Grandpère D'Orsay had mentioned to him was here on Canal Street in many guises and uses. A clown wore a short nose that elongated itself at the owner's will when he pressed a hidden spring. A girl wound a spring and became a Musical Powder Box, with children following her for blocks. There was a man with a face like a clock, with hands that snatched at passers-by. Startled merrymakers squealed and retreated, then screeched as an old maid on stilts bore down upon them.

"I've never laughed so much in my life," people were saying.

It was fun to be with the boys from Monsieur Blont's School. But even strangers were fun. They yelled, "Hello, Pirate!" or they shouted, "Look out for the bold, bad pirate; he's dangerous!"

In and out of the crowds, sometimes pressed against a decorated window and sometimes whirled out to the curb, Pierre went the whole length of Canal Street, from Bourbon to the river. He lost track of the boys.

Much as he enjoyed the flamboyant carnival, he was glad to be on the levee. The carnival boats had docked, and a banana boat was in from South America. Strangers found it odd to look up at a boat, but for Pierre it was the usual thing. The river was higher than the city and was held back only by the levees.

Banana carriers, hoisting great bunches of green bananas from the hold of a ship, moved along a conveyor. Giant Negroes lifted the heavy bunches with as much ease as though they were bouquets of flowers and carried them to the box cars on the near-by tracks.

An old Negro woman, a basket on her head, peddled refreshments to the Italians and Greeks working on the levee.

Pierre bought a sandwich and sat down on the grassy bank to watch. Someone sat down beside him. Billy Moffet again! He had a triumphal gleam in his eyes.

"Tell you what," he suggested, "if you don't want to sell me that old hat, let's wrestle for it."

"No, thanks," Pierre said. "I studied fencing, but I'm not much of a wrestler."

"Nothing like trying." Billy rose and wove about.

As Pierre got to his feet, Billy gave him an unexpected shove that sent him sprawling. But Pierre was up again like a flash. Billy attempted an upper-cut to Pierre's jaw, but Pierre was not there when the blow was ready to land. He had not learned to evade a rapier thrust for nothing. This was fun, this defensive fighting.

Billy Moffet, however, had no intention of letting Pierre dance about him like a fencer. He lunged towards him, his arms outspread, and enveloped him in a bear hug. The boys went down, rolling over and over. Pierre's arms were pinioned, but he kicked with his legs. Billy yowled, and Pierre yowled himself, fighting for breath.

"Enough of this, young fella!" A heavy hand lifted Billy by the scruff of the neck.

"Josef!" Pierre scrambled to his feet. "How did you happen to be here?"

The Praline Man did not answer. His gesture was as plain

as the one word, "Get!" and Billy Moffet *got.* Pierre realized that Josef must have been following him for some time.

"Whew!" Pierre brushed himself off with relief. "He certainly did want my hat. . . . Where *is* it?"

Pierre's cry was a wail. The Praline Man handed the hat to him.

"Here it is," he said. "I took it away from young Moffet." And then he was gone before Pierre could open his mouth to say thank you.

Pierre straightened his clothes as best he could, adjusted his mask and hat, and set off for the bank above the circle where he was to meet the family for a picnic supper. Seated at last, he gazed at the fine figure of General Lee atop the column and waited for the parade of Comus, the last parade of the Mardi Gras and the one for which New Orleaneans always felt a special fondness.

Swift, ecstatic shivers ran up his spine, and he tingled with a great and wonderful joy as he heard the music and saw the glittering parade approaching under the flaring yellow lights of torches carried by red-robed Negroes. Fairy palaces rose to ethereal heights, strange lands and strangely beautiful people lived on the floats—fairies, ogres, witches, kings and queens! The air was white with confetti, and the snowy curtain enveloped the whole scene in an unearthly beauty. This was the world of fantasy that Grandpère D'Orsay had loved, the world of opera that they all loved. Carmen lived, and Hansel and Gretel, and Parsifal—and, of course, *Les Huguenots.*

At midnight, when the bells of Saint Louis rang out, the

Mardi Gras was over. It ended on the exact stroke of twelve. The world of fantasy was suddenly gone. The palaces turned back into papier-mâché, and the most beautiful fairy on the floats turned into Collette.

Back in the house on Royal Street Tante Bébé waited in the double parlors. The grandmothers and Tante Evangeline had retired by the time Pierre and Collette returned with Papa and Mama. Mammy Margot whisked the sleepy Collette off to bed.

With Tante Bébé was the Coin Collector. He picked up Pierre's hat as Pierre pulled it off wearily and laid it down on a table.

"My guess was right," said Monsieur, the Coin Collector. "The decorations on the hat are real gold pieces. I have, in my research, discovered them on velvet costumes and in necklaces. Quite often they were worked into the designs of exquisitely woven baskets."

Pierre's drowsiness was dispelled by the word baskets. He knew now why the Praline Man had followed him—it was the hat he was anxious about—and why he was so eager to receive his gift of the baskets. Gold pieces woven into baskets! That was the answer.

But where were the baskets? With the will?

CHAPTER 13

Saints at Noon

EACH festival brought with it a spurt of better business for the Pirate Pastry Shop, but each rise was followed by a slump when the holiday was over, and after Mardi Gras the D'Orsays were especially discouraged. It wasn't that people didn't eat enough cake; they did, but it was the bread sales—the staple output of the shop—that never reached the desired peak. Distinguished people coming home at midnight from the French Opera often stepped into the Pirate Pastry Shop for some delicacy. Many tourists who came to view the French Market and to have a country dinner of boiled beef and horseradish at Tujague's came in to buy a dessert of frosted cakes and chocolate éclairs filled with rich custard. But that was all the lighter side of the trade.

Pierre was sitting in the back room of the shop one evening, waiting for his father to close the ledger. Papa had said no word about selling either the house or the desk as yet, and Pierre was silently wishing that no word would be said until spring. In the meantime, if the pastry shop could be made to yield greater profits, maybe even the spring deadline would be postponed. They would surely find the will sometime.

It was Monsieur Boudro who put some of Pierre's thoughts into words, though his worry had quite a different angle.

"What we need," the baker complained, "is more common trade, the garden variety. We need customers that we can depend on day after day, every day, world without end, amen."

"Where would we get such a trade?" Pierre inquired.

"From the Quarter! Where else?" Monsieur Boudro shrugged his shoulders. "Neighborhood trade! They all need bread."

"I wouldn't worry," Papa advised. "None of us is going hungry, though there are many hungry ones in the Quarter."

"They will be fed tomorrow," Monsieur Boudro affirmed. "Have you seen the evening paper?"

"I glanced just at the headlines," Papa said.

"In the headlines is not the news of the poor and needy, but of the great, like President McKinley!" The baker opened the bulky newspaper to a back page. "Behold! Tomorrow is the Feast of Saint Joseph, the patron saint of the poor. Many families will have feasts in his honor and will turn no hungry person from the door from sunrise to sunset. At noon they will feed the saints, then distribute what is left among the needy."

"Feed the saints?" Papa was trying to recall the custom.

"At noon, Papa," Pierre reminded his father. "A family

feeds the hungriest children of the neighborhood first. If there are only three, they represent Joseph, Mary, and the Christ Child. They are the saints, and they may have what they wish from the feast that is spread."

"Yes, yes." Papa remembered now. "The feast is given in gratitude, for some favor the family has prayed for. But I've heard that a good many poor families impoverish themselves to carry out a solemn promise."

"Ah, Monsieur D'Orsay, you have said what was on my lips to say." The baker gave a huge sigh. "I know such a family."

"So that's what we're getting at!" Papa's mustache twitched. "Tell me about them."

Without hesitation Monsieur Boudro began, dramatically, to spill out his story.

"They are very, very poor. They live in a little shotgun house on Dumaine Street near Anton's restaurant where your father used to dine among the common peoples on a Saturday night. May he rest in peace, your sainted father who loved the poor! who gave to the poor! The son of my friends is very sick last year—very sick. The neighbors come in; they cannot help. The relatives arrive; they cannot help. They bring the doctor; he cannot help. No help! They pray to Saint Joseph who knows the heart of the poor. They pray long, they pray earnestly, with all their hearts, *but* . . ."

Monsieur Boudro spread expressive hands. He shrugged his shoulders, first one, then the other. Pierre sighed almost as deeply as the baker. It was dreadful to think of a saint hesitating.

"But Saint Joseph did help them." Pierre tried to hurry the story along.

Monsieur Boudro looked at him reproachfully. He wanted Monsieur D'Orsay to savor the full flavor of the tale. Majestically he switched into the historic present.

"The son of my friends, little Enrico, may die. The papa and the mama offer a bargain to Saint Joseph. The papa say, '*You* do this *for me,* Saint Joseph—you save my little Enrico—*I* do this *for you:* I give a Saint Joseph Feast that cost *fifty dollar!*' "

"That's a good deal of money for a poor family to save in less than a year," Papa observed.

"They have not *quite* all of it," Monsieur Boudro admitted. "Cakes and bread for maybe twenty-five hongry ones would make all that is required—even left-over stale bread and cake would be welcome."

He cocked his head on one side like a robin and looked at his employer.

"What are you waiting for?" Papa demanded gruffly. "See if you have enough left-over bread and cake for twenty-five people. Give them what you have on hand and bake more if necessary. Hear me?"

"Monsieur! Monsieur!" What a wealth of gratitude and admiration Monsieur Boudro could pack into an exclamation of delight!

Pierre feared that the baker might kiss his father, which would be embarrassing.

He flew here and there, getting out boxes and wrapping paper, counting "little breads" and yard-long loaves, and bringing forth from the cases the finest of brioche and cakes. Setting into the pirate boxes such éclairs as even the Pirate Pastry Shop seldom baked! Even Pierre noticed the extra thick chocolate frosting.

"We seem to have more left-overs than usual," Papa observed.

"Maybe I bake a little more than is usual," Monsieur Boudro admitted. *"Bread cast upon the waters:* it shall return to you, Monsieur D'Orsay."

"After many days," said Papa, amused. "Pierre, perhaps you will enjoy helping Monsieur Boudro with his burden. I understand that after the saints have dined, the rest of the food is given to the poor. That amount of bread should fill quite a few stomachs. Well, they are welcome to it."

Such a load! Monsieur Boudro was twice as wide as usual when he squeezed himself out of the shop with boxes tucked under both arms. Pierre carried the long loaves, his two arms scarcely able to encircle them.

Pierre and the baker crossed over through Pirate's Alley which was much wider than the banquettes. Even the people who lived in the Quarter and were used to carrying bundles stared after the pair. On Chartres, after passing the Cathedral, people stepped into the gutters, to make way for the burdened ones.

The small, inconspicuous house before which Monsieur Boudro halted was as unlovely as an old shed. Pierre knew at once what it would be like as he had been in shotgun houses before, one room back of the other along a narrow hall. The front room of this one was a shoe repairing shop, as the sign in the window indicated.

Pierre hoped the hall would not be too narrow.

Neither he nor Monsieur Boudro could reach the bell, but

they managed to get up the well-scrubbed steps and kick at the door. It opened immediately, and a small, dark man with an instantaneous smile cried, "Come in, come in—and Welcome!"

The callers wedged in, and a slim, handsome boy with sparkling black eyes relieved Pierre of part of his bundle.

"Mama!" the boy shouted. "Come quickly! Never did you see so much bread!"

"Coming, Enrico!" answered a singing voice.

So this was Enrico! He led Pierre into the front room which, except for this one night and the next day, was the shoe shop. It had been transformed into a shrine.

The dining room table had been brought in, and on it a fine white tablecloth had been spread. At one end, furthest from the door, were the colored statues of Joseph and Mary and the Christ Child. The background was of azaleas, camellias, and roses. From the kitchen in back the odors of good food filled the narrow hall and the shop.

By midnight the feast would be spread, even though the saints did not dine until the following noon.

Already the table held several large cakes and dishes of pyramid-like small cakes made of tiny squares stuck together with a rich, congealed syrup. Neighbors who were helping with the cooking came in, bringing a red snapper on a platter, stuffed and baked, and decorated with watercress, olives, and lemon slices. Enrico's mother added a pan of artichokes with meat filling, tomato sauce, and melted cheese. Other relatives and friends donated olive salad, candied yams, and dishes of colorful oranges, bananas, and pomegranates.

"Have you ever been hungry, Pierre?" Enrico inquired.

"No, never," Pierre answered. "Sometimes I have had a good appetite, but I have never suffered from hunger."

"Come tomorrow noon then, please." Enrico made of the invitation a request for understanding. "The three saints who will eat our feast have been hungry almost always. For longer than I like to think, they have been living on bananas from the mart."

Pierre knew what that meant. He had seen old men and

bent shawled women and ragged children waiting for the shippers to discard the ripe bananas that would not stand distance hauling. The day's freedom from want depended upon how many bananas were thrown into the immense can provided for the purpose. Many a time Pierre, coming from the French Market, had seen some kindly dealer add a generous number of bananas to those in the can at the curb.

"They will enjoy the good bread." Enrico's brilliant eyes thanked Pierre more than his words. "All the neighborhood will be grateful."

"Please," Pierre begged. "Do not tell the neighborhood. My father would not want that. He gave only the left-overs for one day."

Enrico did not contradict with words, but his smile, pleasantly crooked, showed that he did not accept Pierre's explanation.

At school the next day, Pierre could scarcely keep his mind on his work. There was a half holiday, because among Monsieur Blont's pupils were several boys whose parents were prominent Italians.

Just before noon Pierre found himself hurrying along Dumaine Street, looking for the little shotgun house. It was now marked by a green bough tacked into the runway, and every house in the Quarter where a feast was to be held had a similar sign. The green boughs were visible on St. Philip and St. Ann and St. Louis, too.

By running the last block and a half, Pierre reached the

shoemaker's house just as the Cathedral bells were striking the noon hour.

In the hall, sitting stiffly on a bench, were two boys and a girl, in shabby, clean clothes. The boy closest to the door smiled at Pierre.

"Are you a saint?" he inquired, moving over to make room on the bench.

"Oh, no." Pierre's smile embraced the group. "There are only three saints to be fed this noon. What is left will go to the poor, you know."

The boy hesitated, then he said, "If you're very hungry, you may take my place. You see the Pirate Pastry Shop gave Enrico so much bread that we were fed both last night and this morning."

Pierre, embarrassed by this information, refused politely and made his way back through the crowds of curious tourists who had come to view the feast and to contribute to the Poor Box. Somehow he could not stay and stare at the hungry children.

Only a few days later, Monsieur Boudro noticed that the bread sales had increased. He requested Mama to bake extra batches of brioche, but nearly always at the close of the day he was sold out. It was unbelievable.

Monsieur D'Orsay had been called to the plantation for a few days, and Monsieur Boudro hoped with all his heart that the miracle would last until he returned.

"It is like magic," Monsieur Boudro said. "The bread cast upon the waters has returned after such a little time."

Pierre and Collette were as mystified as their elders.

The Return of the Bread

COLLETTE D'ORSAY took a long breath as she turned the corner at Canal and Royal Streets. The main thoroughfare of New Orleans, known as the widest business street in America, never seemed so crowded as that one short block on Royal, with its newsboys, its arcaded markets, its oyster bars, and its curio shops. Mama had decided that Collette was grown up enough to go out walking without Mammy Margot, and she was having a lovely time. She told herself that when she crossed Iberville, she would stop off in Solari's just long enough to straighten her hat.

As a matter of fact, she could no more have passed Solari's than a thirsty child could pass a bubbling fountain. The program was always the same. Once inside she viewed the fruits and vegetables first, the big limes, the out-of-season berries, the white cauliflower, the new peas, and the giant oranges. The cheeses in queer wooden boxes or tinfoil always attracted her: Roquefort from France, Edam from Holland in tulip red balls, and Cheddar from England. There were meats and fowl, and there were delicatessen salads that tempted the eye. The store smelled always of full-bodied coffee being ground, of vanilla and spices and fresh oysters.

Most wonderful of all was the olive barrel. It was the biggest olive barrel in the world; of that Collette felt certain. No matter how many were sold, it was always over half full of big, succulent olives, floating in a mouth-watering brine.

Today Collette heard a sigh of admiration beside her. Another little girl was looking into the olive barrel, a slim child with bright black eyes in a heart-shaped face. Many washings had dimmed the color of her red dress.

"They're wonderful, aren't they?" Collette remarked.

"Wonderful!" the little girl echoed. She asked, shyly, "Aren't you Pierre D'Orsay's sister?"

"Yes. I'm Collette D'Orsay. Do you know Pierre?" Collette inquired.

"But, of course," the little girl responded. "I am Dori, Enrico's sister. It was your family that made our Saint Joseph Feast a success. To think you are the daughter of Monsieur D'Orsay who runs the Pirate Pastry Shop!"

Dori looked at Collette as though she were a Mardi Gras Queen, and Collette, who carefully avoided any mention of her father's excursion into trade at the School for Young Ladies, felt an honest uplift of spirit.

The two girls walked along Royal Street, sometimes pressed against the windows of the antique shops by the pedestrians on the narrow banquettes, sometimes forced into the narrow street. They stopped to look at the crystal bottles in the window of René's tiny shop and to sniff the ever-present fragrance of magnolia. It was said that the front of this hole-in-the-wall shop and the stones of the gutter were swabbed every night with the perfume of this sweet-scented flower.

At Pirate's Alley, Collette agreed to accompany Dori on her errand to the French Market to buy filé for the caretaker of the Ursuline Convent.

"If you have time to go along," Dori promised, "I shall show you the new baskets my uncle has bought. He has the basket stall in the French Market."

"I *am* interested in baskets," Collette confessed, but she did not tell Dori why.

Dori bought the filé, a powder of sassafras leaves, while Collette waited for her at the basket stall. When he was not waiting on customers, Dori's uncle, a dark, lively man, showed Collette his choice stock. Because she evinced so great an interest, he told her of baskets he had seen, so finely woven that they could be folded like cloth. And when she displayed delight in decorations, he told her of the gold pieces from Peru that were used in the designs.

Priceless baskets, he said, had been secured by privateers sailing under the Colombian flag and preying upon Spanish commerce. They brought the loot from the ships they scuttled to the cove of Grande Terre or Barataria where Lafitte and his men sold it to New Orleaneans. It was nothing short of legal stealing, of course, he added.

Collette felt it best not to mention Grandpère D'Orsay.

With Dori, Collette crossed Chartres again and came in

sight of the Ursuline Convent. Across the street stood Billy Moffet eating a praline.

Collette tried to keep her eyes and her mind on the convent. The story of the coming of the nuns from France was familiar to her. Those brave ones had been six months on the ocean, living through storm, sickness, and the fear of attack by pirates. They had come to be the first teachers and nurses in the new colony of Louisiana, and the convent had been built early in the 1700's to house them.

"The Mother Superior's name was Tranchepain." Collette spoke her thoughts aloud. "That means 'slice of bread.' People must have thought for a long time that bread is very important."

Her sidewise glance told her that Billy Moffet had noticed her and was crossing over.

"Bread's the staff of life," Dori affirmed solemnly.

"Hello, Mamselle D'Orsay!" Billy called out.

"Bon jour," Collette responded politely.

"Can't you talk United States?" Billy sneered.

"*Mamselle* is not United States," Collette retorted. "Surely you know that in the Quarter 'Good day' is *Bon jour*."

"Sounds snooty to me," Billy decided, "as if you had plenty of prosperity—just around the corner. This part of town is certainly run down, but the Governor wants me to see it so I can tell about it in school. That convent certainly looks as though it had seen better days."

Collette noticed the soil on the plastered walls that had once been so smooth and white, but the windows were still beautiful in design; and the high brick walls gave privacy to the garden enclosure.

"Grand'mère Jaculi says that the oleanders in our patio," Collette offered, to show Billy he didn't know everything, "are from slips that the first nuns brought from Martinique. Every oleander in the city, for that matter, came from the first slips."

"Interesting, if true," Billy shrugged, not in the least impressed.

He followed the girls into the grounds, looking about at the shrubbery. Dori pulled the bell cord of the custodian's cottage, and a colored girl came to the door to take the filé. She said the old convent was wide open because workmen were repairing some of the plaster. . . . Yes, they might go in if they chose.

As Collette turned from the door, Billy said, "Say, are your folks going to sell that desk or not?"

"Not!" Collette snapped.

"What price are you holding it for?"

"We're not holding it for a price—and please don't bother me any more."

She seized Dori's hand, and together the girls ran into the convent. At the base of the winding staircase Collette stopped to look at the wide, hand-hewn cypress boards of the floor and the wide treads of the stairs. She laid her hand on the cool, iron rail of the handsome, curving stairway and asked, "Could we go to the top floor? I've never seen it, and that's where the young nuns lived when they first came to Louisiana."

"We may go," Dori said. "The caretaker says we may."

Suddenly Collette heard Billy at the open door. He had followed her and was shouting, "Hey, there!"

The girls looked at each other, and without a word, started to climb. Billy surely could not hear their gentle steps.

The stairs were shallow, easy to climb. The last, very old nun who had climbed these same stairs had seen, from the windows on the top floor, the flags of five governments unfurled in Jackson Square. Collette's excitement mounted as she climbed upward on the worn treads of cypress. Soon she would look out the window, and in her mind's eye see them all, one after another, over the years: the three golden lilies on the white banner of Louis of France! The golden castles and red lions on the ensign of Spain! The yellow and red striped flag of Hispañola when the bar of Aragon was added! The exciting tricolor—God bless Grandpère D'Orsay—of Napoleon's France! Last and always, the Stars and Stripes of the United States of America!

Dori and Collette had reached the top floor. Collette, breathless with eagerness, said, "Oh, please let me open the door!"

It took all her strength to push it in. The weight on the rope was unusually heavy.

But now the two of them were in the long, wide hall, with the white-plastered cubicles opening on either side. While Dori ranged up and down, Collette stepped into one of the little rooms. It wasn't such a little room after all, and it had an oddly slanting ceiling and walls. There was one

large, beautiful window, deeply recessed in the thick wall and looking out on the world.

Here had lived some gentle little nun from sunny France, here in the quaking heat of tropical summer and the chilly rain of the delta winter. Through terrible pestilences of bubonic plague and yellow fever! Through constant threat of Indian massacre! Through family tragedies that left many orphan children in her care!

She must have had a wonderful, calm spirit. Collette tried to imagine it all as she went from one chaste room to another. There were no furnishings left, only a few pictures of saints tilted against the white walls.

Sunlight slanted across the floors before Collette realized that it was time to be home from her stroll. When she came to open the door, however, she could not so much as move it a crack.

"Put your shoulder against it, too, Dori," she begged in alarm.

Push as they would, the two of them together could not budge the great door.

"It couldn't be locked!" Dori turned wild, frightened eyes to Collette. "There is no lock."

"Something's against it," Collette reasoned.

"The workmen!" Dori decided. "One of them must have set his tools against it. They were repairing the stairs."

Dori and Collette ran back to a window overlooking the quadrangle. Workmen and gardeners had gone home. The Presbytery was empty. Even the caretaker had disappeared.

Then Collette heard a familiar laugh, and Billy Moffet came out from behind some bushes.

"Hello, Mamselle D'Orsay!" he called. "What have you to say for yourself?"

"Billy Moffet, you come right up here and let us out," Collette demanded.

"Certainly—for a favor," Billy agreed.

"What favor?" Collette asked impatiently.

"I want to know what price your folks are holding that desk for," Billy answered.

"I've told you the truth," Collette fumed, "and that's that."

"Think it over," Billy said airily. "If you don't change your mind before I reach the gate, I shall keep right on walking."

"Then keep right on walking!" Collette yelled.

"I don't blame you," Dori sympathized. "But now what are we going to do?"

Billy Moffet had gone on down the street without looking back. But passing the open gate were several small boys from the neighborhood.

"Lucien! Anaise! Donald!" Dori called. "Help us!"

The small boys consulted with one another. Perhaps, their grins seemed to say, Dori was fooling.

"Get down the way you got up!" Lucien shouted.

"We can't," Dori wailed.

"Come along, fellas," Anaise said distinctly.

"Donald!" Dori's cry was a shriek. "Collette D'Orsay is here with me, Collette whose papa runs the Pirate Pastry Shop!"

The little boys froze to attention.

"Let's see her," they demanded.

Collette rose on tiptoe beside Dori and called down, "I am Collette D'Orsay. Please come up and open the door. Something has been placed against it."

She had hardly spoken when she heard the pounding of feet on the cypress treads.

"Notice how the three words, Pirate Pastry Shop, act like magic?" Dori asked.

"But *why?"* Collette inquired. "Tell me, please."

"Because the Pirate Pastry Shop gave to our Saint Joseph Feast," Dori explained.

There was the scraping sound of a chest being moved; Billy had filled it with tools. Finally the door swung open.

"Thank you," said Dori to her neighbors.

"You're welcome!" Lucien bowed in mock courtesy.

"Thank you," said Collette.

"You're double-welcome," Anaise declared.

"We've been buying bread from your papa's shop," Donald put in, "ever since Saint Joseph's Day."

"You *have?"* Collette was beginning to understand what Monsieur Boudro had called a miracle. "Then it is you who are our new customers."

"All of us," Lucien assured her, "and our neighbors. We do not forget."

Collette ran nearly all the way home. She rushed through the small door in the big, green gate, tripped along the brick runway, and finding no one in the patio, swept up the steps to the main floor of the house, shouting, "I know who is buying the bread! I know who is buying the bread!"

Mama, with the grandmothers, Tante Evangeline, and Pierre was in the back parlor.

"Who?" everybody asked at once, staring at Collette's flushed face.

"The Italians!" Collette was still shouting. "The wonderful, the grateful, the kind Italians who cannot forget the bread Papa gave them on Saint Joseph's Day."

" 'Bread cast upon the waters,' " Grand'mère Jaculi murmured softly, and Mère smiled in agreement.

"I found out something more, too," Collette boasted, as Mama asked her to lower her voice. "I found out that baskets can be so finely woven that they can be folded like cloth and put away in a small space."

"Would you suggest a hiding place, cherie?" Pierre teased.

"Well, if the Napoleon desk had had secret drawers," Collette decided, "I think it would have been a good place."

Everybody was laughing as Mammy Margot announced dinner.

CHAPTER 15

Spring Fiesta!

VISITORS had been flocking into the city for days. Colonial and ante-bellum homes were opened to the public, and young women of the old families—and the young men too—got out their handsomest costumes and strolled on their lawns beneath the dark magnolias and waving palms. A procession of endless carriages and cars viewed the flowers; and groups strolled in silken grandeur through Pirate's Alley and into the Pirate Pastry Shop on Orleans Street.

Live Oaks, as one of the most famous plantation houses, was ready to receive its northern visitors and guests. Both grandmothers and Tante Evangeline had gone to the country to help Tante Bébé prepare for the festivities, but Papa stayed in town, because, for this one week at least, he was needed at the Pirate Pastry Shop far more than at the plantation.

There were always roses in New Orleans but the azaleas had bloomed early this year. Northern and western visitors exclaimed over the great oaks in Congo Square, the royal palms on Rampart Street, and the patio shrubs, the purplish trees of redbud, the scarlet incas, and the yellow-gold parkinsonias. Visiting children carried sweetbuds in their handkerchiefs, and every woman opera patron wore a camellia or a cape-jasmine in her hair.

Pierre and Collette were having spring vacation. Pierre had passed his examinations and now spent most of his time at the pastry shop. Each day he and Collette put their heads together in an effort to think of a new place to search for the will. Papa, however, worried over finances, for he realized that the Spring Fiesta would bring the last spurt of business before the heat of summer discouraged tourists and sent many old patrons to the mountains. Thus far he had kept even with his obligations, but if business fell off a great deal during the summer months, he would have to get rid of the Royal Street house. Selling the desk might provide temporary relief.

He had been deeply touched by the loyalty and gratitude of Enrico's and Dori's friends, they who had sent the bread sales soaring. To Pierre he said, "They have already repaid me. Tell Enrico and Dori to ask their friends to go back to their former bakers."

Although Pierre delivered the message, the bread sales continued to be good. The cake sales mounted, too, during the Spring Fiesta, for the many tourists liked the pirate boxes so well that they shipped gifts of cakes to their home towns. Monsieur Boudro's delight should have proved infectious, but Papa was in no mood to respond. His concern swung like a busy pendulum between the pastry shop and the plantation.

Paul Crager was about to get his degree in medicine, and Lotta was busy preparing nourishing meals for him and seeing to it that he got some sleep. More than once she expressed her satisfaction at being able to make things comfortable during the last difficult months of her husband's training.

"You have earned our deepest gratitude," she said to Papa one evening when she was helping him with the books. "And you have proved to your father—to Grandpère D'Orsay—that you have business ability. You took a forlorn hope and made it into an enjoyable reality. Even Marie Fortier, who had lost faith in herself and her work, has had a taste of success. But do you know what she is going to show at the Spring Fiesta?"

"I couldn't guess," Papa said.

"Portrait of a desk!" Lotta exploded. "Imagine! When she can do such wonderful portraits of people! If she wanted to do a still life, why didn't she do some camellias or magnolias, or even a rich grouping of the various oranges grown in Louisiana—Mandarins, Satsumas, navels and kumquats! Or a stall of vegetables in the French Market! But—a piece of wood!"

"Have you seen the portrait of the desk?" Papa inquired.

"I've been too busy to run up," Lotta confessed.

"I haven't seen it either," Papa admitted. "But I have seen the desk. It has personality, as Marie said. Pierre saw the portrait and was much impressed."

"But is he any judge?" Lotta questioned. "After all, he is a very young man."

"Old enough to recognize a masterpiece," Papa insisted. "The desk is the very best work of a fine cabinet maker. If Marie Fortier has recorded the spirit of his work, her labor may be well worth while. There are pieces of furniture so proudly created that they are signed with the names of their authors."

"Yes. I know."

"If Marie chooses to hang her portrait of a desk in Pirate's Alley, she must have a reason."

If Marie did have a reason, she did not let the public know. By noon of the day set for the display, dozens of artists had hung their pictures. Both sides of Pirate's Alley, the Cabildo side and the Cathedral side, were like a picture gallery. Pictures ran along Cabildo Alley and all the length of the garden behind St. Louis', then around to Royal Street.

It was on the cathedral garden fence on Royal Street that Marie hung her picture. Having hung it in the middle of the fence, it was plainly visible from Orleans Street.

The cathedral garden fence on Royal Street was not considered a choice place. Pedestrians coming and going often shoved against spectators who stood gazing at a picture in quiet enjoyment.

Several times Pierre saw Marie, standing outside the Pirate Pastry Shop, where she was helping Monsieur Boudro, and pointing out the picture on the fence. Between themselves Pierre and Collette decided that Marie had painted the picture mostly out of gratitude, to advertise the shop and to remind people that here the desk had been stored, the desk that was to have been the gift to Napoleon.

No one was much surprised when, on the second day of the fiesta, Mr. Moffet and Billy appeared in the shop with Madame Moffet. She was a stout, fair-haired woman, superbly tailored—Marie said, "superbly upholstered." But her tiny, beautifully shod feet hurt her. She announced this fact in the same breath that she asked to speak to Miss Marie Fortier. Monsieur Boudro was in charge of the counter at the time.

Taking it for granted that the Napoleon desk would be hers, she announced that she intended to bid for the picture during the auction, to be held on the final day of the Spring Fiesta. But first, she wished to ask a question: why were the purple shadows used? and why was the detail work of the diamond-shaped inlay work etched in so distinctly?

The desk, she recognized, was the original desk of a fine cabinet maker, and she did not doubt that the D'Orsays had the actual antique. Monsieur Boudro was glaring at the officious woman as Marie came in from the street.

Madame talked about the desk at length; then she informed Marie that she was living at the Pontalba and that she wished to discuss the details of buying the desk with Monsieur D'Orsay at his leisure. She was certain that the price could be adjusted.

"Won't you come upstairs to see the desk?" Marie invited. "It is on the top floor, and I am sorry that we have no elevator."

"I simply couldn't climb three flights of stairs," Madame Moffet explained.

"Monsieur D'Orsay would not like you to buy 'sight-unseen,'" Marie persisted.

"I am satisfied!" Madame Moffet snapped. "I have seen the picture—I mean the portrait."

Her face colored even under the perfect make-up. Then hastily she ordered some little cakes and macaroons for tea. To be delivered before five!

"Would you mind," Marie asked, "having Master D'Orsay bring the cakes over so that he may talk with you?"

"Not at all!" Madame's face lit up with pleasure. "I should be most pleased."

She left with her silent escort.

"It is plain," Monsieur Boudro decided, "that she rules the roost."

When Pierre came into the shop later in the afternoon, he found Marie relieving Monsieur Boudro.

"Pierre!" she cried. "Here is a box of cakes for Madame Moffet. She will be most pleased to see you. This is your chance to try to dissuade her from buying the desk. If you succeed, I am sure we shall be able to tide over for your father. Those were her exact words—*most pleased.*"

"I'll be most pleased myself," Pierre said.

He whistled as he walked along Orleans Street and through Pirate's Alley, whistled to keep up his courage.

The address, he noted, was on the second floor of the upper Pontalba Apartments. There was no elevator service there, Pierre reflected, but it was just like Madame with her love of antiques to have chosen to stay in one of the oldest apartments in America. Perhaps she even imagined herself the Baroness Pontalba, who had caused the building to be erected; or Jenny Lind, who had sung from its galerie.

Yet Madame had refused to climb the stairs in the Orleans house. She seemed to be perfectly sure of the desk, as if she had memorized every turn of the carving. Josef must have been pretty close to being right then: it was Mr. Moffet who had taken the sketch. Mrs. Moffet couldn't be so sure just from having seen Marie's portrait.

Pierre went in through the tall doors and climbed the graceful stairs, his hand on the smooth rail, perfectly designed for boys to slide down. Up and up and curving around!

A maid let him into the Moffet apartment, taking the box of cakes from him. He had called with Mama in the Pontalba Apartments before, but he had never seen one quite so handsome. The floors of cypress had been rubbed to a shiny dark brown, almost black, like those at home and on the plantation. Inside shutters folded back and fitted into the frames of French windows, set in the eighteen-inch-thick walls. Up in the fourteen-foot ceiling a chandelier glittered, its prisms dancing rainbows.

In the black marble fireplace with its trim of elaborate wrought iron, a small wood fire blazed. Candles of myrtle burned fragrantly, as if to create a mood. An alabaster vase of yellow roses stood on the tea table.

As Pierre went slowly towards the blooms, he heard the

rustle and swish of silk and turned to face Madame Moffet in her handsome rose-colored frock. It spelled Paris—Worth's.

"Madame Moffet?" Pierre bowed. "I am Pierre D'Orsay. Miss Marie Fortier sent me."

"You are Pierre D'Orsay?" Madame lifted her lorgnette and stared at her caller. "But I expected your father. Miss Fortier must have said *Master* D'Orsay. I thought she said *Mister*. I do not wish to hurt your feelings, but I should scarcely wish to discuss business with you. Did you bring the cakes and the macaroons?"

"Yes, Madame," Pierre answered. "But may I speak with you just for a moment?"

"Sit down." Madame seated herself and indicated a chair for Pierre.

"Madame Moffet," Pierre began earnestly, "my grandfather's desk that he bought for Napoleon is very dear to us. You could easily have a duplicate made."

"So I could." Madame's tone was sarcastic. "Young man, it may interest you to know that I do not buy duplicates. I buy only originals."

"There may be another original, as you call it. Perhaps the cabinet maker turned out more than one desk of this design."

"Heaven forbid!"

"Then you do not really like the desk?"

"I think it's an atrocity. The wood is elaborate enough without all those diamond-shaped inlays—like too many ruffles on a dress."

"Then why do you want it?"

"My reason for purchase—I don't know why I'm bothering to explain this to you—is purely commercial. That wild story of yours concerning your grandfather's connection with the Napoleonic plot will double the price. Rich people are often sentimental."

"We D'Orsays are sentimental too, Madame."

"You're old enough and big enough, Pierre D'Orsay, to have a little sense," Madame Moffet declared, rising. "There's no place for sentiment when a family needs money as yours does."

Pierre rose, too. The interview was over. But there must have been some understanding in Madame's heart because she asked, "Will you have a cup of tea before you go?"

"No, thanks," said Pierre.

There was a lump in his throat and no desire to slide down the smooth, beautifully curved bannisters.

As Pierre came back through Pirate's Alley to Royal Street, he saw only one man looking at Marie Fortier's picture. Why, it was Papa!

"If we can't keep the desk," Papa said, "maybe we could buy the picture."

Grand'mère Jaculi was right: Creole men were dreamers.

Auction Day!

All during the Spring Fiesta Collette, in pantaloons and billowy ruffled silk skirts, a big flowery hat tied with blue satin ribbons under her round little chin, had been helping friends with their entertaining. People from the North exclaimed over "the quaint child" and invited her to partake of cakes and tea with them. Rather than offend her Yankee visitors, she had accepted too many delectable refreshments.

Finally Mammy Margot put her to bed with a little headache and a slight temperature. Mama gave her plenty of fruit juices, but Mammy Margot used her own cure—a *cagout*. The *cagout* was made of cockroaches sewed up in a little piece of woolen cloth and laid under Collette's high-posted bed. Magically, Mammy Margot explained, the *cagout* would do away with Collette's illness and she would wake refreshed.

Mama, discovering the *cagout,* scolded. Why should Mammy Margot indulge in such superstitious practices when she had a grandson who was a doctor? The cockroaches had eaten through the cloth and escaped. Collette, after her good sleep and rest from rich food, was feeling lively and happy; and Mammy Margot insisted, grandson-doctor or no doctor, that the cockroaches had run away with the sickness.

Everybody ate a very light breakfast because Mammy Margot was to serve a regulation Creole "dejeuner" at eleven o'clock. Then the family would be able to enjoy the two o'clock auction. There were just the four of them at home on Royal Street—Papa, Mama, Pierre, and Collette. The aunts and grandmothers were still on the plantation, and Nonc was away on business.

The meal was served formally, course by course. In neat calico dress, fichu, and snowy tignon, Mammy Margot herself brought on the food, serving Papa first as had always been customary. Anchovies and celery livened the appetizers; then came a potage, a clear, tasty soup. The beef and potatoes were served with a green garden salad, the lettuce "fatigué" or wilted. The main course consisted of broiled chops, buttered broccoli, and tiny browned potatoes.

For dessert Mammy Margot had made one of her famous meringues filled with light, sweet custard, flavored with vanilla bean. A bowl of fruit and nuts was placed on the table, after which Pierre and Collette were excused while Mama and Papa enjoyed *un noir,* "a black." Papa said he wished Nonc were home to enjoy the most delicious cup of coffee ever dripped in a New Orleans household.

It was after the elaborate "dejeuner" that Papa followed Mammy Margot into her kitchen, something he rarely did.

"Mammy," he said, "I've got a little something to say to you."

"Madame D'Orsay, she done said it awready." Mammy Margot sulked. "Sour juice ain't made Missy Collette well: *cagout* done hit, bless de Lo'd!"

"I won't argue with you about *cagouts,*" Papa said gently. "What I want to say is this: you can't feed us the way you've been doing on the money I've been giving you since the Pirate Pastry Shop opened. How much have you spent of your own wages? That's what I want to know."

"Why, Massah D'Orsay!" Mammy Margot rolled her eyes, and her round, black face took on the look of a hurt child. "Whar yo' think Ah done been raised thet Ah cain't manage on all the money yo' done gib me? Yo' let me take keer o' this heah kitchen, an' yo' take keer o' yo'r shop. . . . Yo' bothahs me, a-fussin' like thet, Ah 'clar!"

She shunted him out of her domain like the autocrat she was. Papa realized that he could do nothing to make amends to the faithful old servant who would carry on as long as she had a cent herself. The Royal Street house was as much her home as theirs. Long ago she could have gone to live with her children or her grandchildren, but she remained steadfastly loyal to her trust and still called the D'Orsays her "sweet people."

Pierre was waiting, impatiently, for his father in the patio. They walked quickly along Royal Street, but the moment they turned the corner at Orleans, they stopped dead still in astonishment. There was a crowd in front of the

Pirate Pastry Shop, and people were laughing and pointing at the grillwork across the third story of the building.

A boy, in attempting to get over the spikes that separated the galeries, had caught a pant leg and could not climb over.

Pierre, squinting into the sunlight, made a laughing discovery.

"It's Billy!" he shouted. "Billy Moffet! . . . Hey, Billy, what are you doing up there?"

Billy's face looked red even from the banquette.

Collette, who had been given permission to take a walk after lunch, came running out to meet her father and Pierre. Then she glanced upward and gave an exultant cry of triumph.

"Come and help me!" Billy was begging. "Please hurry!"

"Let him stay there!" Collette shouted. "Serves him right!"

"Collette!" Papa had never been more severe with his daughter. "That's no way for a little lady to talk."

"But he left *me* on the top floor of the convent," Collette reminded her father. "We ought to leave *him* up there."

Papa thought otherwise.

"Go ahead, Pierre, and get him down!" he ordered. "What under the sun he's doing there is beyond me."

Pierre dashed into the shop and up the stairs of the D'Orsay building. He knocked on Marie Fortier's door. She let him in, asking, "What's the matter? You've been running."

"There's a marauder trying to get onto your galerie from the house next door," Pierre announced. "Come and see!"

He climbed out of one of Marie's dormer windows, and she climbed after him.

"Why, it's Billy Moffet!" she cried.

"I can't hang on forever," Billy complained. "Can't you hurry?"

Pierre swung his legs over his own galerie grillwork, grasping the railing and edging himself along on the narrow ledge, far above the heads of the growing crowd. When he reached the far side of the screen, he climbed onto it, holding to a cross-bar with one hand and grasping Billy with the other.

Marie crawled back into the studio and shoved her small stepladder onto the galerie. Then she climbed after it and held it steady against the pronged screen.

"Step over on this, Billy," she instructed, "as soon as Pierre loosens your trouser leg."

The cloth was so firmly wedged into the ironwork, however, that Billy could not free himself even when Pierre steadied him.

"Cut the cloth," Marie suggested. "Shall I get my shears?"

"I have a pocket knife," Pierre said.

He had to pass the knife down for Marie to open, because he had to hold onto the grillwork. Then, holding to the long prongs, he made a slit in Billy's pant leg. Freed, Billy stepped tremblingly over onto the ladder, carefully avoiding more prongs; and Pierre edged back along the galerie and climbed back to safety while the crowd below applauded.

Collette, her face red and angry, pounded up the stairs to Marie's studio. She burst into the room where Billy stood blubbering.

"Serves you right!" she stormed. "I wish they had left you there a long, long time."

"It seemed long as it was," Billy confessed.

"Here, I'll sew up that rip the jackknife made," Marie offered.

"Don't you do it!" Collette yelped. "Let his pants stay torn."

Marie got out her thread and needle, saying, "I'm only going to snap the tear together. I don't fuss for marauders."

Billy was so embarrassed that his face was red into his collar.

"I just wanted to see the desk," he sniffled and reached

for his handkerchief. "Gaston told me it would be easy to climb over."

"So Gaston did tell you," Pierre said. "Too bad he didn't get caught with you. But now you're here, look at it—and then go home."

Billy just barely glanced at the desk behind the easel.

"Don't know why anybody should make such a fuss about that old thing," he said.

"I *told* you not to be nice to him," Collette accused Marie.

Billy followed Pierre down the stairs. Suddenly he realized that he was very unpopular and he did not relish it. Miserably he stood around the pastry shop, striving to strike some note of friendliness.

"Why do you call New Orleans the Land of Dixie?" he asked Pierre wistfully, trying to make conversation.

It was an unbroken tradition that New Orleaneans must be genial and polite to strangers. Pierre belonged to this tradition, provoked though he was.

"I'd show you," he relented slightly, "but I have to deliver some cakes on Canal Street."

"I'll go with you," Billy said hopefully, and since Pierre didn't answer, he took it for granted that he was welcome.

The errand on Canal Street swiftly done, the boys turned back on Royal Street, and at Iberville Pierre pointed up at the cornice of the old building at which Billy was staring and said, "That's it. That's the building that was occupied by the Citizens' Bank that issued the Louisiana banknote called a 'dix' and worth ten dollars. . . . Money was plentiful in New Orleans before the Civil War. Ten dollar bills were as common as nickels are now, I guess. Strangers called our city the Land of Dixies."

"So that's what I'm whistling when I make music," Billy said with a chuckle. "'In Dixie Land I'll take my stand!' I thought I was whistling about patriotism—south of the Mason-Dixon line, or something like that. Had no idea 'Dixie' referred to money. Speaking of money, have you changed your mind about selling me that hat with the funny decorations?"

"Those funny decorations are worth dixies and you know it," Pierre said. "Better spend your money at the auction."

"I will," Billy decided.

He slowed his steps only long enough to gaze at the St. Louis or Royal Hotel. With Pierre he looked at the magnificent dome and frescoes, and went in to see the winding stair. Then the boys took a look at the great hall downstairs, paved with black and white marble where stood the slave block.

By the time they reached Pirate's Alley the auction had begun. The auctioneer had set up a table and stood with his back against the Cabildo Alley wall, his mallet pounding out his sales. Beside him, amused, stood a handsome young man in tweeds, with a portfolio under his arm. From time to time this young man made a note or two.

"Ladies and Gentlemen," the auctioneer announced, during a pause between sales while his helpers bought him more pictures, "we have with us as our guest, Mr. Robin Landry, an authority on art and antiques. His comments will be published in tomorrow evening's papers."

"Hope he has plenty to say about the desk," Pierre whispered.

"He'd better, if my mother buys it," Billy confided. "She needs the publicity to sell it."

"I was talking about the picture," Pierre explained coldly, "and your mother may *never* buy our desk."

"Says you," Billy taunted.

The bidding went forward. Portraits, sketches, etchings, and impressionistic paintings went over the auctioneer's table to tourists, townspeople, and art dealers. When the "Portrait of a Desk" was lifted for public view, Pierre and Billy both regarded it nervously. The auctioneer seemed puzzled.

" 'Portrait of a Desk,' " he read, turning the picture over. "By Marie Fortier. Obviously, Ladies and Gentlemen, it *is* a portrait of a desk. A very pretty desk at that! What am I bid?"

There was a brief pause.

"Fifty cents," Pierre called out, suddenly remembering his promise to Marie.

"Young man," the auctioneer observed good-naturedly, "the paint in the purple shadows is worth that."

"Five dollars!" Billy shouted.

The bidding was sporadic, but it kept up. The auctioneer was plainly astonished at the number of bids, for more people were peering at the picture. Papa and Mama were there in the background as if to lend moral support, but they did not bid. Madame Moffet herself was holding back, knowing that her interest would send the price soaring. Someone was bidding for her; Billy frankly admitted it.

It was no surprise, after the picture had sold to a strange gentleman, to have Madame Moffet come up to the two boys and announce that the "Portrait of a Desk" was hers.

"I am lending it for a window display to the Royal Antique Shop," she said. "Would you take it over for me?"

"I'll be glad to," Pierre answered politely.

"Okay," said Billy.

"Did you notice," Madame asked, "how closely Mr. Landry studied it?"

The critic was still examining the picture when the boys went over to the auctioneer's table with Madame Moffet's receipt. He seemed loath to let them take it away.

"I should like Marie Fortier's address," he said, "if she happens to be a New Orleanean."

"She lives over the Pirate Pastry Shop on Orleans Street," Billy informed him. "You can see the shop right from Pirate's Alley if you step out into it."

"She has the desk in her studio," Pierre volunteered. "My father owns the building in which she has her studio. My Grandpère D'Orsay bought the desk to give to Napoleon."

"My mother's going to buy the desk," Billy boasted.

"It's the work of a great cabinet maker," Mr. Robin Landry pronounced. "Most unusual piece! Most unusual drawers!"

Someone touched Mr. Landry on the shoulder, and he turned away.

Most unusual drawers! Pierre looked more closely at the "Portrait of a Desk" in his hands. A startling thought came into his mind, so startling that his heart beat with wild excitement.

CHAPTER 17

The Secret of the Desk

PIERRE was so elated as he hurried home to tell Collette of his startling idea that his walk kept breaking into a run. Everything around him had taken on a new and exciting beauty.

The Quarter was exceptionally attractive in the spring. The purple wisteria on the roof across the street spilled bloom. The cool, crisp flowers of the pomegranate tree in the Cathedral Garden were one mass of orange-scarlet, fluffy as the skirts of ballet dancers. Glancing into a patio as he rushed along Royal Street, he saw a mimosa tree, buds bursting early into white fluff; and somewhere, hidden behind a high wall, waxy magnolia was sending its sweetness into the narrow streets. People were chattering over a vase of scarlet oleanders in a French Book-store. It was strange how many things you noticed when you were keyed up.

He banged through the small door in the green gate of the Royal Street house but found no one in the patio. In the kitchen, on the ground floor, Mammy Margot was singing a spiritual in her rich, black plush voice. Standing in the doorway a moment before she discovered him, he saw something he had never noticed before, a can near the stove filled with "spills" of rolled paper, used to save matches. Although it was dusk in the low, poorly lighted kitchen, Mammy Margot had not turned on the lights, she who loved brightness.

And was that plate of stale left-overs to be her supper?

Pierre walked boldly in, picked up the plate, and inquired, "Cat food?"

"Yo' ain't been raised with no mannahs lak' thet!" Mammy exploded. "Put thet plate down, do yo' heah? Yo' knows well's me the cats is all on the plantation an' the dogs too."

"Maybe a cat is coming visiting," Pierre teased.

But he did not feel like teasing. If his startling idea didn't work, there was no telling how impoverished the household might become. He saw Mammy Margot heaping their plates and eating scraps herself. He saw his father burdened with the expenses of the Royal Street house, about to lose it to creditors. He beheld Monsieur Boudro working day and night to keep the Pirate Pastry Shop going, but hopeless to carry the D'Orsay obligations. Before the immensity of the problem, Pierre's elation evaporated.

"On my way home, Mammy Margot," he confided, "I thought I had a wonderful idea. Now I'm afraid it won't work. I'm almost afraid to try it for fear it will fail."

Mammy's busy hands were rolling little pancakes in jelly and almonds for dessert. Mammy herself was far away in her thoughts.

"Cheri," she advised, "nevah be 'fraid of an idea. Hit's thinkin' makes the wo'ld go 'round, God thinkin', me thinkin', yo' thinkin'. Ain't anythin' without thinkin'. Yo' go ahead with thet idea. . . . An' speakin' of cats, I ain't nevah had no time fer fraidy-cats."

"Thanks, Mammy. Will I have time before dinner?"

"Yo' *take* time, Massah Pierre. Ah'm gettin' old: Ah kin tarry."

Pierre ran into the house, shouting, "Collette! Collette! Where are you?"

Collette was ready for a stroll, waiting for Tante Evangeline to finish some sewing.

"Come with me," Pierre commanded. "I want to show you something."

Collette, trotting beside her brother, said, "It must be something wonderful."

"It's got to be wonderful!" Pierre affirmed.

In front of the Royal Antique Shop, to which he had delivered the "Portrait of a Desk" less than an hour ago, he paused. The dealer had set Marie Fortier's picture in the window, and a placard announced its loan by one Madame Moffet.

"Look at it!" Pierre commanded. "Look hard!"

"I've seen it before." Collette's voice faltered in disappointment.

"Look hard!" Pierre commanded again. "Stand back and squint at it."

Collette squinted while pedestrians passed between her and the window.

"Funny," she pondered, "but those little groups of diamonds on either side look like little drawers."

"That's it!" Pierre shouted. "You're warm, Collette. That's it! They *are* drawers, secret drawers, I do believe. That's what Mr. Robin Landry must have meant when he said that the cabinet maker who built this desk was famous for unusual drawers!"

"But they haven't any handles or pulls," Collette objected.

"I know it," Pierre acknowledged.

"Then how would they open?" Collette demanded. "That's what I'd like to know: *how* would they open?"

But Pierre, deep in memory, was back at Anton's with Nonc Samuel. He was sitting in a room steamy with food odors and he was saying, "Do you remember my grandfather's ever telling you about how he hid things?" And Anton was answering, "Once he say he have magic spring—he touch—voila! Suddenly a little box appear."

"Well?" Collette was shaking Pierre's arm. "How *would* they open?"

"By magic springs," Pierre answered with a far-away look. Then becoming suddenly alert, he repeated it. "By magic springs!"

"But where are the magic springs, Pierre?" Collette questioned.

"That's all we have to find out."

"All?"

"Well, it can't be too hard."

Walking to the Pirate Pastry Shop, Collette made only one more observation: "It's queer, I think, that we didn't notice that a group of diamond inlays looked like a drawer when we saw the desk. Yet we noticed it, both of us, on the picture."

"That's because Marie Fortier is a real artist," Pierre decided. "She accented those inlays, even without knowing how important they are—or we *think* they are. She must have seen them through the eyes of the cabinet maker."

Marie was in the shop waiting on customers while Monsieur Boudro and Annette frosted a wedding cake. She said certainly Pierre and Collette might go up to her studio and have another look at the desk. They knew where to find the key.

Pierre made the steps two at a time. Collette was beside him when he pushed the door in.

"Let's go at it systematically," he suggested. "Let's look all around the outside first."

"Maybe one of the diamond inlays itself is a spring," Collette guessed.

"You take the diamonds," Pierre directed, "and I'll take the rest."

He began to feel under the desk.

"That's silly." Collette was laughing. "You couldn't expect an emperor to get down on his hands and knees to open a desk drawer."

"He had servants," Pierre said scornfully, "lackeys to do his every bidding."

"You read a book," Collette snapped.

The outside of the desk showed no betraying mark to

either Pierre or Collette where a spring might be concealed.

Next in his systematic search Pierre examined the large, lower compartment. Collette followed over every surface with her exploring fingers. All the surfaces were silky smooth.

"That leaves only the drawers above the working surface," Pierre mourned, "and they are empty!"

"Couldn't they be empty and still have springs in them?" Collette inquired.

"You think of everything," Pierre observed with brotherly scorn.

"There's a little, round knob here," he said, "to make the drawer slide more smoothly, I suppose. . . . No! It presses in!"

Even as he spoke, a group of cemented diamond-shaped inlays sprang out like a jack-in-the-box!

"It's a drawer!" Collette gasped. "It's a secret drawer!"

Pierre was even more astonished than his sister. He was actually astounded. There, in the border of the left-hand side of the desk, stood a fair-sized drawer.

"I feel sort of foolish," he acknowledged, "to think we didn't discover it before."

"Let's see what's in it," Collette suggested practically.

"Your hand is smaller than mine." Pierre glanced in. "Hand the stuff out to me."

Though both of them were thinking of the will, neither of them spoke of it.

Collette had thrown aside her hat, and the big blue bow

on the chocolate brown curls was trembling as she reached in.

"There's plenty!" she announced. "I can feel something soft like cloth . . . and something hard like coins . . . and something like paper, I hope."

First of all, she drew out a package tied with a silken cord.

"Three soft, pliable baskets with the same decorations as the Mardi Gras hat!" Pierre counted. "They are marked: 'For Josef Garavalia, Friend in Need.' "

"Something else. Small boxes with names on them, and they are very heavy." Collette lifted off a cover. "Gold pieces! I never, never, in all my life, knew there were so many gold pieces."

"Leave the covers on!" Pierre commanded. "We must deliver them as they are."

"I know how King Midas felt," Collette confessed.

She brought up a handful of necklaces, some handsome jeweled bracelets, and a number of sparkling rings. She slipped a bracelet over her little wrist, put on a number of rings, and tossed a necklace over her head.

"You look like a Christmas tree!" Pierre declared.

"I feel like a Christmas tree!" Collette cried. "I feel as if I had everything exciting and lovely in all the world."

"Except the will," Pierre reminded her." It must be in there. Here! Let me look!"

Pierre delved into the secret drawer, and his smile faded.

"No will," he said.

"There must be another drawer," Collette guessed.

"That's our only hope," Pierre decided.

He opened the drawer in the upper part of the desk again, felt for a spring on the opposite side, and pressed it. Like magic a drawer in the diamond paneling on the right-hand side of the desk sprang out.

Pierre could not resist glancing in at once. He could feel his eyes lighting, color coming into his cheeks, joy flooding over in his heart.

Collette peeked in too.

"You pick it up, Pierre," she begged. "Please."

Wordlessly Pierre obeyed.

Now the document was in his hands.

"It is the Last Will and Testament of Grandpère D'Orsay," he said, quite simply.

For a moment Pierre and Collette stood looking at each other quietly, so overwhelmed with their good fortune they could hardly believe that what they held in their hands was real. It was real, though, and with a shout of joy Collette began dancing around the room, brown curls bobbing up and down, and the jewels around her neck sparkling gaily. Pierre held the will high in one hand, grabbed his sister with the other, and together they pranced around chanting, "We found it, we found it."

They didn't even hear the door open as Marie came up to investigate the noise. But she didn't have to be told what the excitement was about; she saw for herself.

"Marie, dear Marie," Collette called when she saw her and ran to throw her arms around her. "It was all your picture, Marie, that gave Pierre the right idea."

And they both began explaining how they discovered the secret.

"We thank you, chère Mademoiselle," Pierre said in his best gentlemanly voice, as he bent to kiss her hand.

"Oh, it is wonderful, children, and I am so glad. The D'Orsays deserve good fortune," she said. "And to think it was here all the time."

Collette was ready to fill her arms with treasures and run home to show the family, but Pierre didn't see how they could carry everything through the streets.

"Let's just take the will and the baskets, and come back for the rest later," he suggested.

"Can't I just wear this necklace?" Collette begged.

"All right." Pierre couldn't say no to anyone just then. "But let's get everything else back into the drawers so we can discover it all over again for Mama and Papa." Marie helped them pile the things back into the secret drawers, and then they dashed home as fast as they could go. No lighter feet ever raced past Pirate's Alley.

CHAPTER 18

The Will

So much talk and so much excitement happened during the rest of that glorious day that when Pierre woke up the following morning he thought at first that it had all been a dream. Then he heard Mammy Margot singing, no sobbing spiritual, but a wild version of *Dixie,* and he knew that every bit of it really had happened. He raised his voice to join Mammy in the chorus:

Hooray, hooray,
I wish I was in Dixie,
Hooray, hooray.

It was a wonderful day for the D'Orsays, and they made the most of it. Mammy Margot was busy with a "comp'ny dinnah," and not even Mama was allowed in the kitchen. Pierre came again and again to the doorway of the kitchen to stand and admire the goings on. But he didn't dare step in.

Monsieur La Branche was coming to dinner with the family as he had that other night that seemed so long ago.

This was to be a real festive occasion and no doubts about it. Nonc Samuel whistled as he dressed for the evening and finally appeared in the parlors, smelling of shaving lotion, fine tobacco, and good coffee.

"Good evening," he said jovially. The grandmothers, in their best black silks with rosepoint lace at throat and wrists, smiled at him in answer, as they rocked side by side. Tante Evangeline, in a pale pink frock, was arranging a low bowl of camellias, but Tante Bébé fluttered near the French windows, watching out for Papa and Monsieur La Branche. Pierre and Collette walked proudly from room to room. They had truly helped Papa save their home and had a right to be proud.

"Here they come," Tante Bébé announced from the galerie window, and a few minutes later Monsieur La Branche was bending over Mama's hand and Papa was saying, "So we're together again under one roof."

The supper feast was typical of the gracious living the Royal Street house had always known. Mama, in her stiff blue silk dress and with jewels in her hair, smiled across the camellias at Pierre and Collette, a very special smile that thanked them. The family was together—and happy.

After supper, just as on that earlier and more solemn occasion, everybody gathered in the parlor. When the family was comfortably settled in a semicircle, Monsieur La Branche took his place before them and began:

"I do not need to recall Grandpère D'Orsay to you today. I dare say Grandpère D'Orsay has been with all of you in thought these past few months—less than six—more than he ever was in his lifetime. Although he is gone, we have had to deal with him. . . . Shall I read the will in detail?"

"I hardly think that is necessary," Papa said, "especially the first part about realizing the uncertainties of this transitory life."

"Very well." Monsieur La Branche turned the pages of the will. "Certain investments go to Solidelle, as she already knows, and the plantation, known as Live Oaks, becomes the sole property of Pierre D'Orsay—Senior—his heirs and assigns. . . . Description of property follows. There is no mention of the Orleans house, I might add, since that property had already been an unconditional gift."

"A christening gift," Mère specified. "I believe Samuel was provided for handsomely some years ago."

"That is true," Nonc Samuel stated. "Grandpère D'Orsay invested in my business."

"Only one other item, or I should say, group of items, may concern us at this time," the lawyer continued. "There are three baskets, as you know, intended for one Josef Garavalia, known familiarly as the Praline Man, 'for services beyond the call of duty.' . . . Ahem! These baskets as you must realize, if you examine them carefully, are valuable pieces of art. The workmanship is exquisite, the design inimitable, and the decorations are of pure gold coins. If the family wishes to contest this gift . . ."

Pierre and Collette, who had been bored with the whole recital, suddenly sat up and shouted in unison, "No!"

"I think Pierre and Collette express the family sentiment,"

Papa said. "But I should be interested to know what service Josef Garavalia performed for my father."

"He will tell you," Monsieur La Branche surprised everybody by saying. "He will be here later in the evening. The other gifts he will explain far better than I can."

"Monsieur La Branche," Papa inquired, "do you think my father was merely whimsical in hiding the will?"

"No, sir," the lawyer answered bluntly. "He confessed to me, more than once, that he wished his daughter knew more of the plantation and that his son had the courage and the ability to go into business. I believe I have expressed this before."

"No matter." Papa was impatient, and Pierre saw that his father wished to defend his own position. "Didn't he think it took courage and ability to run a plantation?"

"Certainly. But he didn't want you to follow the Creole custom of staying in the rut in which you were born."

"No matter how good a rut it was," Tante Bébé supplied. "He wanted you to get out—be more American."

"Thank you, Mademoiselle," Monsieur La Branche offered.

"And we certainly had an extra lot to do," Pierre spoke up for Collette and himself.

Papa cleared his throat. "If I may interrupt a moment, Monsieur La Branche, I would like at this time to congratulate Pierre and Collette. If it hadn't been for them I might very well have sold desk and will long ago."

Everybody applauded, and Pierre and Collette didn't know they could feel so happy.

The door opened, and Toby ushered the Praline Man in. Josef carried his basket with him and began, smiling, to pass it around. Everybody said, "No, thank you," except Pierre and Collette who could never resist a praline. Monsieur La Branche shouted with laughter.

"No, Josef!" He waved the basket away. "I didn't send for you to bring us pralines. The D'Orsays would like to know what service you rendered Grandpère D'Orsay that was 'beyond the call of duty.' "

"I did no such service," said the Praline Man.

"We'd like very much to know," Papa urged. "And we'd like to know something about the men to whom he is giving these boxes of gold coins."

Josef read the names laboriously, then he said, "There was not one among them who did not risk his life, at one time or another, for Monsieur D'Orsay."

No one said anything, but all waited expectantly. The Praline Man grinned a queer, twisted grin, not without malice, and still hesitated.

"I know!" Pierre shouted. "Josef is afraid we don't want to hear about Grandpère's piracy."

"What makes you say that, Pierre?" his father demanded. "Your grandfather was an honorable man."

"There were honorable pirates in those days," the Praline Man said, speaking very slowly. "And there were dishonorable pirates! Jean Lafitte, New Orleans must not forget, helped Jackson at the Battle of New Orleans. Monsieur D'Orsay became a pirate in truth, when we were attacked on board a ship sailing from Colombia. He fought as I have seldom seen a man fight when the Spaniards came for us. How he could wield a cutlass! . . . And, naturally, he did not hesitate to scuttle the enemy ship after he had secured the loot. It was powerful sweet loot."

"What became of the loot?" Papa inquired.

"Part of it he divided among the men who had fought with him, and part he hid in his retreat in the city here. Privateering had become unpopular, and it would have been hard to prove that the Spaniards had attacked *us*."

"The law was after you?" Nonc asked.

"Yes, sir. And with a vengeance. But Monsieur D'Orsay had the nerve to keep a hat and wear it at a carnival."

"A hat!" Pierre cried. "Why, that's my Mardi Gras hat!"

Suddenly Mammy Margot's voice was heard in wild argument with several strange voices. Nonc went out to investigate and returned immediately, followed by three people. The Moffets!

"So there you are!" Mrs. Moffet glared at Papa. "I went to your pastry shop, Monsieur D'Orsay, and that impertinent baker of yours told me, 'The desk is not for sale!' "

"It is not for sale," Papa repeated quietly, rising to offer Madame Moffet his chair.

"See here!" Mr. Moffet barged forward. "You can't do this to my wife. We have a legal claim on that desk and on the loot your father took from the Spaniards. My father fought with him, but did he get his share?"

"The answer is no," Billy Moffet shouted. "Old Pirate Moffet never got his gold."

"We have the picture of the desk that the cabinet maker

sent my father," Mr. Moffet began, taking a sketch from his billfold.

"That is my picture!" Pierre was on his feet. "That is the picture I left on the counter the day Mr. Moffet came in."

Everybody talked at once until Monsieur La Branche restored order.

"Mr. Moffet," Monsieur La Branche said with elaborate sarcasm, "you go too far when you claim the desk. Give Pierre his picture. There are at least a dozen witnesses who can swear it is his."

The picture was passed over, and Pierre slipped it into his blouse.

"Just the same," Mr. Moffet recovered from his embarrassment to shout, "my father never received his share of the Spanish loot."

Josef stepped forward, and at a signal from the lawyer, spoke: "On the day we scuttled the Spanish ship that had attacked us, I fought side by side with Monsieur D'Orsay. Pirate Moffet was not with us. He was at Barataria. I still have documents to prove it. But he heard of the valuable loot we had taken and he tried to highjack us. . . . Pirate Moffet always resented any favor that Monsieur D'Orsay showed me, and that is probably why he wanted to involve me in what he calls stolen treasure. I have told the truth."

"Your testimony would stand up in any court, Josef," said Monsieur La Branche.

CHAPTER 19

The Pirate Pastry Shop

PAPA was the only cheerful one at dinner time on Saturday evening following the family conference. So long as he lived, he would be sole owner of Live Oaks. As for the Pirate Pastry Shop, he seemed to have pushed it far back in his mind. Could he have forgotten about it completely? In Mama's smiles there was a wistfulness.

As Papa's fork cut into the cream puff dessert with the rich custard filling, he glanced up to see Pierre and Collette regarding him soberly, so soberly as to make him uncomfortable.

"Like to walk down to the Pirate Pastry Shop with me tonight?" he inquired. "We'll say good-by, eh?"

Sedately Collette, in her simple sailor-suit dress, walked on the inner side of the street next to the plastered walls, while Pierre, in his school clothes, kept next the gutters. They felt no sense of festivity as they usually did with Papa.

"Such sobersides!" Papa remarked, but there was no response.

How could Papa look so gay and debonair? How could

his eyes twinkle so and his little black mustache twitch so mischievously? How could he swing his stick so nonchalantly? Saying good-by to the Pirate Pastry Shop was a duty, but surely not a joy.

The three came in sight of the fragrant Cathedral Garden with its giant sycamores and blooming magnolias, each blossom like a huge white tulip. They rounded the corner onto Orleans Street and saw, ahead of them, the familiar sign of the Pirate Pastry Shop.

The building itself was so dark that the galeries looked like jet black lace. But there was pale gold light in the shop that spread a carpet onto the banquette and street. The back room was bright.

"They're all in the kitchen," Papa guessed.

And he was right. As the D'Orsays walked through the shop and into the kitchen, they saw all the tenants at once.

Monsieur Boudro had piled his crusty loaves onto the cooling racks and was decorating a special order of brioche. At the far end of the work table, in her blue smock, sat Marie Fortier, her bright head bent over a bowl of nutmeats that she was sorting. Opposite the baker himself sat the doctor and his wife. The doctor was watching Lotta's clever hands as she cut designs from candied fruits that he chose from the large jar. Annette, at the near end of the work space, sprinkled spice and colored sugar on the brioche.

"Well, well," Papa exclaimed from the doorway, "everybody seems to be busy."

"Yes, Monsieur," said the baker.

The others said, "Good evening," but kept their eyes on their work.

Marie made room for Collette beside her, and Annette offered Pierre a stool. Papa roamed about the room, talking very fast.

"You've all done an excellent job," he praised. "I want you to know that, without your co-operation, I couldn't have carried on. I am deeply grateful."

No one spoke.

"Now I am free," Papa continued, "to devote all my time and effort to Live Oaks, my plantation. I hope you'll all come out and visit. There's plenty of room."

Still no one spoke.

"I hope you have enjoyed this little shop. Now that it is no longer an obligation, I can look back on the experience of running it with pleasure."

When Papa stopped talking, the clock could be heard ticking, ticking. It was a dialogue between Papa and the clock.

Pierre saw all the heads in the kitchen bend lower, and he was afraid Collette might burst into tears. He hoped she wouldn't be such a baby.

"Monsieur D'Orsay," Dr. Crager said, "Lotta and I want to tell you that being able to maintain a home here in this house has helped us over the hardest period of our lives. Now that I have my degree and can start practicing—I already have an assistant's position—I can pay my rent in cash. Lotta and I would both like to donate our services to the shop, until such time as it closes."

"This house of yours, Monsieur D'Orsay," Marie Fortier said with a rushing eagerness, "has brought me good fortune too. I shall gladly pay my rent in cash from the first of this month, and I want to donate my help in the shop just as the Cragers are doing. My 'Portrait of a Desk' will pay a good many months' expenses. And to think I still have the desk with me is an inspiration!"

Monsieur Boudro said not a word. He slid a pan of brioche into the oven and made a great rattling with his fire.

There was so great a sadness in the room that was usually so merry that Pierre could stand it no longer.

"Papa," he inquired abruptly, "did you ever give me a christening gift?"

Papa stopped pacing.

"What did you say?" he asked.

"I just wanted to know if you ever gave me a christening gift," Pierre repeated.

"Come to think of it," Papa said in an amused voice, "I don't believe I did. It was a most happy occasion, your coming, but I don't remember bestowing any special gift on you. Would you have liked a christening gift, cheri? Seems to me that at one month you could scarcely have appreciated it."

"I would appreciate it *now*."

"Are you hinting for something?" Papa still looked vastly amused.

"Yes, sir. I guess you might call it that."

"Well, out with it. What do you want?"

"I'd like *your* christening gift—if you want to be through with it."

"You'd like *my* christening gift." On Papa's face was pure, unadulterated astonishment. "Why, *my* christening gift was this Orleans house."

"With the pastry shop," Pierre amended.

"Oh, Papa, please let him have it." Collette got up and bounded towards her father. "It would be such fun for Pierre."

"And what would you do for a christening gift, cherie?" Papa inquired.

"I'd like the desk," Collette decided.

Laughing, Papa turned to his son.

"Just what," he asked, "would you do with this building if it were yours? You can't sell it, you know, because it is part of the D'Orsay estate and supposed to stay in the family."

"I know that," Pierre said. "Well, first of all, I'd let Monsieur Boudro go on running the bakery. I'd keep the rest of the tenants, and as I grew up, I'd help more and more. For the present, I'd go on delivering."

No one spoke, but every ear was tuned to what was happening.

Monsieur Boudro lifted from his oven a pan of perfect brioche, decorated with Lotta's candied fruit, Marie's choice nuts, and Annette's colored sugar. But he did not lift his eyes to Heaven and sniff the deliciousness as he usually did.

He spoke for the first time since he had greeted the D'Orsays.

"The last order from the Pirate Pastry Shop," he said, "is as good as the first."

"What do you mean, 'the last order'?" Papa demanded. "This is the first order under new management."

All the heads lifted. All the voices shouted. All the bent shoulders straightened.

Pierre said, "Surely, Papa, you can't mean it! I was only doing a little wishful thinking."

"You'll have to do more than that with a business on your hands," Papa decided. "I don't want you in a rut, helping me with the plantation. I want you to have the courage and ability to do things the American way."

The three D'Orsays walked home on Royal Street, Pierre and Collette as gay and debonair and nonchalant as Papa. Pierre could hardly contain himself. The Pirate Pastry Shop was his. Papa would help him though and Mama and Collette and all the dear people who lived in the Orleans house. Felix, too, would come in from the Bayou country, and the aunts and grandmothers and Nonc would all be a part of it. He wove them all into his dream.

"As long as grandfathers do whimsical things," Papa said, "like buying desks for exiled emperors and hiding wills in secret drawers, fathers will do whimsical things like giving businesses to very young men."

"As long as people are hungry for bread," Collette said, "bakers like Monsieur Boudro and boys like Pierre will see that they get it."

"As long as people come through Pirate's Alley," Pierre said, "there will be a Pirate Pastry Shop to welcome them."

THE END